# My Chunk
## of a Century

*Moments that Mattered*

Carol Poe Straubinger

iUniverse, Inc.
New York   Bloomington

My Chunk of a Century

iUniverse books may be ordered through booksellers or by contacting:

iUniverse
1663 Liberty Drive
Bloomington, IN 47403
www.iuniverse.com
1-800-Authors (1-800-288-4677)

ISBN: 978-1-4401-5067-8 (pbk)
ISBN: 978-1-4401-5068-5 (ebk)

Printed in the United States of America

iUniverse rev. date: 8/18/2009

# Acknowledgments

I am deeply grateful to my granddaughter Gail Mikels, who donated her time and computer skills toward publishing this autobiography. I thank Lois Santalo for showing the way, and I credit my sisters, the Poe girls, for the head start provided by sixty years of Round Robin letters and for contributing their memories of growing-up years back on the farm.

# Contents

# A FATEFUL MOMENT

That she would never again see him alive was the last thing on Mama's mind that fateful morning, March 28, 1930, when she kissed Daddy goodbye and turned to her work. He had hitched his rather skittish new team of horses to a wagon filled with grain and headed to the town grain elevator.

We four older girls were in school and little Alyce was playing with a doll as Mama settled down to finish making some Campfire Girl skirts. The happy hum of the treadle sewing machine was interrupted by the ringing wall phone, a short and two longs, our party line signal.

Uncle Henry's grave voice delivered the shattering blow, "Olive, there's been an awful accident: Stanley has been badly hurt. Grace is on her way to come and get you." Thelma Ewing, a next-door neighbor, came onto the line with, "How can I help, Olive? I'll be right over." To this day, Alyce remembers Mother's uncontrollable crying. "What's the matter, Mama?" she kept asking, but there was no answer.

Not until our thirty-one-year-old mother was in Aunt Grace's car headed for McComb did she learn that her beloved husband was already gone, killed when he rushed to stop his newly-bought horses who had not yet learned instant obedience to his "Whoa!" Daddy was caught between the wagon bed and an elevator beam. He was instantly crushed to death.

Uncle Henry's next sad task was to collect us girls from our schoolrooms, with the help of a teacher, and take us a short block to

1

join Mama, by now there at his home with Aunt Inez. I can't believe my memory is correct when I recall the abrupt way Miss Roberts broke the news to me.

I was taking a history test when Mr. Slater answered a knock on the door. He looked toward me with utmost gravity and said, "Carol, you are wanted outside." Foolishly, I thought "Uh-oh, I'll bet Uncle Rex has died," not realizing that I would hardly be called out for that. His illness had been much on my mind and he did die two days later.

Sadly, I went out into the hall. There stood the short, trim, brisk Miss Roberts. She wasted no time in giving me her bitter message, "Carol, your father has been killed and you are to get your sister Edna and meet your Uncle Henry in the office." And off she went. This sledgehammer blow froze my brain and jellied my knees, but I managed to stagger over to the water fountain, mercifully only a few feet away. I can still feel the cold, hard, firm reality of that fountain as I leaned on it to get my bearings before carrying out the mission so suddenly thrust upon me. I must have done it in a zombie-like state for my memory is a blank until we were all outside.

Walking behind Uncle Henry on the short block toward his home, Irene and I remember staring fixedly at cracks in the sidewalk, trying to block out the reality of the blow we had been hit with. Our uncle had told Irene and Mary only that something awful had happened. When seven-year-old Edna had been called out of her room, she told a classmate that she was probably going to be taken to an ear doctor.

For once, we could hardly expect comfort from our shattered mother. We found her crying hysterically as Aunt Inez and Aunt Grace brought more and more hankies and a glass of water to keep her from fainting. Like us, Cousin Evelyn was in a state of shock. We sat on a sofa across the room from Mama, all in dazed silence. Edna says she still didn't understand about Daddy until she saw his body in a casket in the big front bedroom back at the farm.

For days, the house was full of supportive, shocked, grief-stricken relatives and neighbors. The floor of the large front room was covered with sprays and baskets of flowers. Later, whenever I smelled carnations I could recall the awfulness of those days. The fine metal and soft, quilted, white-satin lining of the casket held a cruelly unresponsive statue of our Daddy. But where was *he*? The finality of his death was hard to comprehend.

Was our father an especially impulsive thirty-three-year-old man or was it that he had been so distracted at that one fateful moment that he couldn't think straight? After the grain had been emptied into the silo for storage, he was waiting in line to leave the elevator. He had become engaged in a conversation with Cal Culp, a member of a committee planning the upcoming Community Institute. His horses understood that they were to leave the elevator when the wagon ahead moved on. But the men hadn't finished talking at that point. Mr. Culp yelled, "Don't go in there, Stanley! You'll be killed." But it was too late. Yelling, "Whoa!" he dashed for the reins to stop his horses, thereby pinning himself between the swerving wagon bed and an elevator beam, instantly ending his life.

Stanley Poe had been a charter member of the Rotary Club. It was his second year as president of the Community Institute, called the Farmer's Institute before he broadened its scope. By the time a shocking headline in the *McComb Herald* screamed, "FATHER OF FIVE KILLED," with the subhead, "Stanley Poe Crushed to Death," McComb's 1100 residents and farmers for miles around already knew. According to the paper, "One of the largest crowds that ever attend a funeral in this village was present to pay their last respects. It took thirty-five minutes for people to pass by. Between 400 and 500 machines were parked for miles around the church."

Our family had gone to a small country church, but the funeral was held in town at the Methodist Church. Long lines of people paused at the casket to say goodbye to this man who had been such a leader in his community. They glanced sadly toward his grieving widow and five daughters wearing their new Easter dresses for the first time. Alyce had a red-and-white-striped sateen bolero dress. I had a stylish new tweed "ensemble."

By the time the paper came out, my own shock and grief had ebbed to the point that I—silly young girl—felt momentarily famous when I thought, "I'm in headlines. I'm one of the five." I was the oldest one. My twelfth birthday had been just ten days before that tragic accident. With a gush of tears, I recalled the favors Daddy had given each Campfire Girl at my surprise party. He gave each one a can containing a sprout that would grow into a Christmas tree. They were from a plot of sprouts he was growing to sell when they were ready.

There was more violent sobbing as a circle of mourners watched the casket being lowered into the grave. Decades later, my grown-up daughter Donna asked to see where her grandfather was buried. Though Mother had regularly taken flowers there, I had lost interest in revisiting the scene. But as Donna and I stood there, a long-buried memory of that final good-bye came rushing to the surface. I felt again the awful finality of watching the casket go down, down, Daddy gone forever.

Back home, the crowds of loving friends gradually diminished, but spells of spasmodic sobbing behind Mama's closed bedroom door took a long, long time to subside. To be both mother and father to five little girls—Carol, Irene, Mary Lou, Edna, and Alyce—and to manage a 350-acre farm was an overwhelming role for this shaken woman to assume, even one as patient, kind, resourceful, and gifted with motherly wisdom as Olive Blanche Smith Poe. But her valiant spirit moved her forward.

# MAKE-DO MAMA

Even before her bereavement, Mother had had ample opportunity to exhibit her exceptional qualities. As Daddy went about his work, she tended to the house, kids, chickens, and garden with skill and vigor. Her German heritage and her own ingenuity produced mealtime goodies that we Poe girls remember with special pleasure. She baked bread and cookies in a black kitchen range heated by coal and wood. She made noodles from scratch by rolling the dough in big circles, drying them over the backs of kitchen chairs, then cutting them in strips and cooking them in chicken broth.

She churned butter—with a little help from the young-uns. She filled rows and rows of basement shelves with home-canned tomatoes, corn, and green beans from our garden, made elderberry jelly and canned cherries from Aunt Grace's trees, and canned peaches and plums from "boughten" bushels. It was a happy chore to be sent down to the basement to make a choice for supper of one of the fruits.

The cellar also stored crocks of pickles: dill, mustard, chunk, and sweet, and crocks of green peppers filled with sauerkraut. There was always a supply of apples and just once a glorious treat—a box of oranges. The cellar was also our dairy. We had a cream separator, which I usually operated and washed after each use. The cream became butter. Skim milk (then thought to be unfit for human use) went to the pigs to become pork. At butchering time, the cellar was a busy scene indeed with canning and sausage making. On hot summer days, Mama cooked down there on a coal-oil stove.

A huge tub of peanut butter, costing all of fifty cents, provided filling for our standard school lunch sandwiches after being enhanced with honey from our beehives. Dessert was always a cookie and an apple. Bologna was a rare but welcome variation. One Christmas treat was a batch of taffy poured onto buttered platters until it was just the right texture for pulling. Another treat was popcorn balls colored red and held together with sticky syrup. Popcorn itself hardly qualified as a special treat since we had it so often. We kids sat around the kitchen table and ate it from a dishpan while Daddy sat with his feet in the range oven reading as he put away fistful after fistful. In those days, there was never even a grain left in the dishpan.

Roasting ears was a seasonal variation on the corn theme. The pile of cobs in front of Daddy's plate once set a record. Noon meals were not called lunches—they were dinners. The biggest were prepared at threshing time when farmers who shared Daddy's threshing machine went en masse from one farm to another until all the grain was threshed. Those meals consisted of all the best dishes the gathered corps of women could think of in the way of meat, bread, and potatoes, plus pickles, jellies, heavy salads, pies, and cakes. The men washed up in washtubs down at the pump. How they were able to drag themselves back to work after such feasts remains an Ohio secret.

Mama was never able to put together a modest assortment of dishes for special days like Thanksgiving. She had to have both sweet and mashed potatoes, several kinds of pickles, both pie and cake, and so on. Potluck suppers with members of Pleasant Hill Church and family reunions were occasions for all the women to trot out their best recipes. Mama was always sure to bring more than enough and then add still more to the bulging picnic basket.

It must have been more than she could bear, to finish making those Campfire Girl skirts when the shattering phone call came. Through the years, she had made dozens of dresses and nighties for her five girls—even for their dolls. Quilts and doll clothes made use of leftover scraps of fabric. One year when money was tight, those miniature-doll wardrobes became our main Christmas gifts. I remember a tiny coat made of ribbed fabric. It was fully lined—even the sleeves—and it had a velvet insert on the collar. Amazed, I asked, "How could you do this on anything so small?" Mama replied, "What's worth doing is worth doing well." Sewing was probably an expression of art for her.

We wore hand-me-down clothes routinely. In later years, we got some from Aunt Maude, whose well-off daughters discarded quite a few things that had been high style in their time, but seemed merely weird to us by the time we got them. We did get some new clothes, however. The most delightful togs came in time for an annual event, Children's Day at the rose-filled Pleasant Hill Church, one of the few times Daddy went with us. Dotted Swiss and patent leather shoes prevailed. One time when Mama was getting us ready to go and "speak pieces" and participate in dialogues and songs, Daddy mildly reproved her for powdering our scuffed knees. What would have been his attitude when we were old enough for lipstick?

In the winter, our best dresses were likely to be velvet, sometimes combined with a silky fabric. We wore—and hated—long underwear. For Christmas, we were given—and loved—new flannel nighties Mama made for us.

We girls all had jobs to do. Dishwashing was divided among three of us. One washed, one wiped, one "reddied-'em-up-and-put-'em away." We rotated these jobs weekly and debated which of the three was least onerous. Once when Mama went to town and left us to do the dishes, we found a way to procrastinate: the dishwater was put on the range to get hot while we went out to play. But when we returned, the water had gotten too hot, so we went out to play again until it cooled off. When Mama got home, the work was still undone.

Perhaps this was one occasion for use of the switch, a limber twig that rested atop a corner cupboard until it was worn out or mislaid, in which case we would be sent out to get a new one. Opinions differed on whether a thin or a thick twig would sting least and on whether or not it was helpful to have some leaves on it to make a racket and make it seem more effective than it actually was. Sometimes, Mama encouraged better behavior by merely reaching her hand up toward the switch corner.

When she came home from shopping, she usually brought a small white sack of candy. To this day, there is something pleasing about the rustling of such a sack. If someone needed shoes, she had to go along to Findlay with Mama, who would have a list of things to accomplish. But she would often run out of steam before finishing. How we hated to hear, "We'll have to put that one off till the next time."

Dishwashing was only the least popular of our jobs. To clean the house was an endless proposition. Sweeping our kitchen was more satisfying than sweeping Grandma's. We always got a nice dustpan full at our house, but very little at Grandma's. We didn't have running water, unless you count girls running up and down the outside flight of stairs to bring a pail from the well. The stairs and well were icy in winter. Luckily, we did have a pump in the kitchen sink to bring rainwater up from the cistern.

Another job was feeding the chickens and gathering the eggs. It was a challenge to reach under a broody hen without getting pecked. Another job was running clothes through the wringer from the washing machine and from the two tubs of rinse water, and then hanging them out to dry. We worked in the garden and occasionally in the fields with Daddy. Taking our Collie, Laddie, along to get the cows was one of the nicer jobs. Even milking had its charms: the sound of the milk against the side of the metal pail and the fun of squirting milk into the open mouth of a cat or sister. Probably the most popular job of all was feeding an orphan or twin lamb from a baby bottle.

Left to be both mother and father on a 350-acre farm with five daughters to support in 1930 during a depression was a heavy fate for a young woman. In those days, Ohio people, especially hired hands, did not expect women to know much about crops. Perhaps their dislike of taking orders from a woman was the reason hands tended to come and go. In later years when we girls got together, we had a contest to see who could remember the most hands who had worked for us.

The next-to-last hired hand was Bill, a dull, slow, grouchy man. He was greedy at the table and ate noisily with his mouth open. Threat of the switch kept us civil toward Bill, but Ed was not so deterred. Ed was a transient who had come by seeking work. Since he was clearly not a tramp or a "hobo," and Bill was not keeping up with the farm chores, Mother decided to give him a chance. Ed couldn't have been more different from Bill, who resented this vigorous, quick-thinking interloper on his domain.

One can only guess at the irritating last straw that touched off Ed's temper. Our family was sitting around the kitchen table having our Sunday-night popcorn when Bill lurched through the back door with a bloody nose, shouting, "What kind of a maniac is this guy you hired, anyway!" This incident was the last straw for Mother also; she fired both of them and ordered them to leave at once. That was the only time we didn't finish every last grain of popcorn!

Mother set wheels in motion to sell all the farm machinery and move. She bought a small house at the edge of McComb. There were five acres for popcorn, chickens, and a cow. There was a small orchard, not good for much besides climbing. We girls were pleased to trade the school bus ride for a mile-long walk to school. We could swim, play tennis, and socialize with the town kids who would gather in our front yard Sunday afternoons when Mom got out the iron kettle and started popping corn.

Another game we girls played in later years was seeing who could remember the most jobs Mother worked on to make both ends meet. We weren't aware that the country was in the middle of a depression. We thought Daddy's death was the cause of our tight money situation. There had been no insurance, but there was a bank account of about $12,000. Mother was under the jurisdiction of the Hancock County probate department, which required her to spend every cent of this money for tangible needs of her girls, divided equally. She had to keep track of every pair of shoes, socks, or underpants on a separate page for each girl. She regularly had to take the record to Findlay for auditing. In return, she was given a small "mother's pension." Presumably this would provide food and other family needs. Because this was far from enough for food, housing, utilities, and other necessities, she had to get a job. Fortunately, the bank president, against regulations, told his friend, Uncle Henry, to advise Mother to transfer her funds to a Findlay bank. She did. The next week, the McComb bank closed its doors.

Daddy had always done the driving; now Mother had to learn. Even worse, she had to learn to talk with strangers. When I had traveled to the west coast with Mother and Daddy the previous fall, they had no sooner set up camp in the evening than Daddy went about getting acquainted with everyone else in the campground before supper. Seeing him approach with someone to meet "wifey" and his daughter as they were cooking on the Coleman stove, Mama would whisper "Oh, goodness, there comes your daddy with another stranger." Her tone did not indicate joy at the prospect!

Jobs in 1930 were scarce. About the only option required selling things to strangers. Too embarrassed to approach anyone who knew her, Mother drove to Leipsic to sell paper products. She also had a go at Spirela corsets and Avon products. Her final door-to-door experience was with the Christy Company. After selling for a while, she was given an opportunity to earn commissions by going about Ohio's small towns to search for other sales representatives.

Alone except for the hitchhikers she often picked up (not an unsafe practice in those days), she spent nights in "tourist homes"; they were not always pleasant. She would ask to see the room so she could feel the bed for lumps. Once, she was sure the sheets had not been changed. Later on, she said she enjoyed the rolling hills of southern Ohio—and was probably only too glad to leave the girls with Aunt Mae, who had come to live with the family.

Mother and Aunt Inez worked in the school cafeteria for a while. Other students could afford the temptingly fragrant food, but we still ate our peanut butter sandwiches most of the time. Happily, if Mother had forgotten to buy bread, we could buy an item or two. The two cooks then opened the Kozy Korner Kitchen near the school. Their lunches were popular with teachers and business people. They had all the noon business they could handle. They spent afternoons baking; their apricot pies were truly extraordinary. Saturdays, we girls peddled doughnuts. There was no question of marketability, but the business didn't last long. Perhaps the prices were too low, or perhaps they just couldn't handle enough volume to make it pay.

Another of Mama's jobs was at the County Home, commonly called the poorhouse. She got up about five o'clock to go to Findlay in time to cook breakfast for the residents. Then, at long last, she managed to get a satisfying job at the post office, where she efficiently sorted mail and cheerfully served customers. This final position suited her so well that she remained there for many years until she retired.

The most amazing fact about all this is that she kept up her love of good times. She would pile our car full of kids and head for Tawa Creek or the stone quarry for a swim. She often took a load of students to basketball games away from McComb. Only once did I hear her complain that none of them ever chipped in on the gas, though unlike her kids, the others had plenty of spending money for snacks. Most of our good times didn't cost much. We'd pick up some ice and go to Aunt Grace's to make ice cream. The church had "ice cream socials" where people brought gallons of homemade ice cream and cakes to sell for a nickel a serving. There were also weenie roasts, hay rides, and Pleasant Hill class parties held in various homes, where we enjoyed parlor games and singing around the piano.

From time to time, Mama managed to scrape up enough money for piano lessons with Neva Weinland. Perhaps they were paid for out of court-administered funds rather than from her earnings, for she bought me an accordion, Daddy's favorite instrument, with my portion. All the girls grew up with a fondness for singing, from hymns in church to the popular songs at home. Mama used to sing "The Prisoner's Song": "Oh, I wish I had someone to love me …," she would start, and we'd chime in with, "I love you!" Then she went on, "someone to-o-o call me their own." We'd answer "You're mine!"

Down through the years, Mother had several men friends. Tom Farthing probably lasted the longest, but an older widower, Dan Ingold, seemed to be most eager to join the family. This man, one of McComb's wealthiest citizens, courted the children as well as the mother. He took us riding and gave us money to shop in dime stores while he attended to business. Once he took Irene and me along to Columbus and turned us loose in a huge department store with five dollars apiece to spend. In terms of delight, this would be about like giving a present-day child $500.00. But not until all the brood had left home did Mother consider remarriage.

By that time, I had gone off to Bluffton College and then to work and marriage in Toledo. Irene had gone about her missionary calling after a year in Bluffton; Mary had followed her Bluffton year with a stint in the WAC; Edna had become a navy nurse; Alyce had married. Both Grandma and Grandpa Smith had died and Mother was living in their house in McComb until she and Webster Ewing were married. They lived on his farm until illness compelled them to move to their final home in Findlay, a cottage in the Weinbrenner complex for older people.

Mother and Webster had some good times together. They drove to

California every other winter for a while, then to Florida when Webster was no longer up to the long trip. They were active in the Presbyterian Church.

Mom was a charter member of the Critique Club, where she lost any remaining vestiges of shyness and made many friends. She kept track of her far-flung family, with many grandchildren. She never forgot a birthday or an anniversary. Sadly, except for Alyce's family, all lived far away. Until her sister Grace died, they talked daily on the phone.

# GOING WEST (1929)

In another twist of fate, only the year before he died, my father was able to fulfill a dream he had held for many years, going to see his birthplace in Oregon. Most autumns after crops were harvested, he had taken fishing vacations to Canada. The year finally came when he felt justified in this much more extensive journey. Not only would he revisit spots where he had spent many early years, but he would also see what life was like for a few McComb acquaintances who had moved to the West. Had Daddy inherited his father's pioneer spirit? Was he thinking of our moving there too? And he had another dream—he aspired to shoot a grizzly bear in British Columbia!

At the time, it didn't occur to me that my sisters might resent the fact that I, the oldest one, had been given so many privileges, especially this one. Needless to say, I wasn't about to object. I was told I could go along if I learned to eat oatmeal for breakfast. Oh yes!

Our Willys-Knight touring car was rigged into a primitive motor home by hinging the front bench seat so that it would fall back and form a bed. In those days, cars didn't have trunks, so Daddy constructed one to serve as a sort of kitchen with shelves to hold a ham, jars of food from home, dishes, a Coleman stove, and a lantern. The trunk door opened to make a sturdy table. When we pitched the tent next to the car and pulled the flap from one side up over the roof, we had a cozy area in which to get in away from rain. The "kitchen" became a family heirloom. My son David took it to Indiana to use for storage.

For three months, the three of us camped. We rode west at the rate of about 350 miles a day. Mother and I each kept diaries. Only a typed copy of hers remains. I still have mine, written poorly in pencil by that long-ago eleven-year-old.

Only one original scrap of Mother's writing remains: a page listing in exact detail every expenditure on the trip. More than sixty items listed under gas show averages of about $1.30. Six under oil total $14.00, $2.15 for tire repairs, two new tires. (The roads were bad.) Total car expense for the trip was $151.57. There were usually free campgrounds. Once or twice, we paid fifty cents and once we got a "cabin." In Washington, we camped in orchards of friends and relatives.

To fulfill a promise Daddy made to the editor of the *McComb Herald*, he wrote three long letters, all of which were printed in full in the paper. When clippings became too cumbersome to keep, I typed them. It's amusing to compare his version of the trip for the public with my childish selection of amusing or pleasing daily events. I recorded "witty" conversations like this one when a bee got into the car: Dad said, "I'm going to let the bumblebee be," and Mom said, "I'll let him be if he lets me be." I used words like "boy"—as in "boy, was it good!" or "boy, it was hot"—and bedtime terms: "turn in," or "hit the hay." Good food was "swell," a bad tire was "punk."

Drab miles like those through states like Nebraska were livened by Mama's reciting poems, by spotting prairie dogs, and by singing our versions of familiar songs. I was especially fond of Dad's version of the song, "Highways bring happy days when they lead the way to home." The improved, delicious version was, "Highways bring Milky Ways when they lead away from home."

Daddy's letters told McComb's farmers that the West had had the driest summer on record. In Montana, a young man told him that "Dad sowed six hundred acres of wheat and harvested none. Now he's looking for work." What little corn was planted didn't grow over two feet tall. Here's what I wrote about the corn: "It is so small that a bumblebee would have to get down on his hands and knees to smell it." (This was probably from Dad's typical wit.)

His letter writes of roads past Yellowstone: "We encountered some terribly rough roads. Ten to fifteen miles per hour was as fast as one could drive and hold his seat. The frame of one man's car broke in two, and a tourist from California said he came into Montana with five good tires and was just about going out on the rims, liberally spicing his statements with appropriate uncouth interjections. We picked up a wandering barber who gave us all a haircut for the lift."

Wenatchee, Washington, where Dad had lived when he was ten years old, was our first destination. He was amazed by this booming city. "Where there used to be frame one-story ramshackle shacks, there were now several-storied brick and stone structures. Orchards are being cut down to make room for residences." It was still a sea of apple orchards, however—my own favorite Winesaps and Jonathans—plus pears, prunes, strawberries, tomatoes, peaches, Amalga grapes, and Hearts of Gold muskmelons which could be bought for five cents each along the roadsides.

We camped by a canyon where a spring-fed stream ran noisily nearby. We explored other canyons where Dad and his brother Dave used to fish and hunt. We located a family of older Poe folks. With Russell Poe, we rode on a boat up Lake Chelan, an area known as "the Switzerland of America." No roads go there. Black bears are common. We rented a cabin for three days while Russell and Dad caught many trout in the swift Stehekin River. Some weighed seven or eight pounds. Mom and I spent the time getting acquainted with people who lived there, people who farmed and also cleared trails and fought fires for the forest service. Mom and I hiked a tiring two miles up to a waterfall. My diary says it "started from way up high and falls a while, hits a rock, splashes up and falls again, continuing till it reaches the bottom." That was my improvement on "real pretty."

Leaving Wenatchee with boxes of fruit packed for us by friends, we drove north toward Bellingham. Along the way, we deplored large stumps, which Dad said "depress one more than a graveyard. They seem to be nature's scourge to those who would destroy her forests. Many of these stumps will doubtless be standing one hundred years from now. In the meantime, tall ferns and young evergreens grow luxuriantly between them."

On the way to Bellingham, Washington, we watched modern machinery canning several cans of salmon per second. We spent two days with former McComb people. We had a picnic, a scenic ride toward Mt. Baker, and a "reunion" dinner with the two families. Young

Lorell and I roller skated, gathered blueberries, and shelled peas, while Mama washed dishes. After the festive McComb reunion, we climbed a mountain and brought back some snow.

British Columbia came next. Along the Fraser River, we gave a ride to a man prospecting for gold. He showed us how to dip his pan into the muddy water and swish it around to get the clay out until a speck or two of "color" would show up at the bottom. We kept on prospecting after supper and he gave us a sample for a souvenir. We drove on an extremely narrow road to a ranch near the mouth of a creek where Dad found the trail for his long-anticipated bear hunt. He climbed fifteen miles, partly beyond the trail, but came back greatly exhausted two days later with a mountain goat instead of the grizzly. He gave most of the meat to Mrs. Simpson and the other friendly residents in the house. While he was gone, I had enjoyed playing checkers with a man there and reading Mrs. Simpson's catalogues and *National Geographic* magazines. She hadn't been out of there for twenty years. I didn't notice at the time, but I'm sure Mother must have been worried sick all the time Dad was gone.

It was raining heavily as we continued our northward journey, with Daddy still hoping to bag a grizzly. About a hundred miles past Ashcroft, we had dinner and then debated whether to continue on. Here's my version: "As we were in a kind of lane Daddy headed out and said whichever way the car went we would go but it didn't go either way but just went straight ahead so we put it to a vote and most voted go back so we did."

Back in Bellingham again, Dad looked at a seven-acre property for sale along with some other farming country. Then we especially enjoyed two days exploring Seattle: beautiful houses, elevated streetcar tracks, roads and sidewalks, and curio shops filled with everything imaginable. We went to the docks to watch lumber being loaded on large freight ships. One ship unloaded tubs of halibut.

Daddy was born in Detroit, Oregon. Visiting Detroit was a highlight of our trip, though he was only three when his family left there. His father had homesteaded 160 acres of virgin forest. When I was very young, I had seen a framed photo of their log cabin on the wall at Uncle Dave's. The cabin was rather indistinct and I thought it was a bench there in front of the very tall pines. I thought, "Why would they take a picture of a bench?"

For many years, Dad had looked forward to the moment when he would finally see his birthplace, about which his parents and older siblings had shared so many memories. He was greatly disappointed that there was no trace of the old cabin or the dugout where they had gone to avoid falling trees when there was a big storm. An old-timer could still point out to us the empty spot Grandpa had cleared. As Daddy sadly described it, "Only two or three tall trees near the cabin site have somehow escaped the lumberman's hand, and they are half dead from the inevitable forest fires that followed the slashing."

Only recently had an auto road been completed to this valley, but thirty years ago, "a railway running into this country up the Santiam River had by fair means and foul forced the homesteaders to give up their valuable timberlands to them for a fraction of their real value and then slaughtered the giant trees to their own greedy satisfaction." Daddy quoted this from a newspaper article and added, "Although I was too young to remember anything of this country when we left, I have heard so much of it that I can't help being sickened by the devastation."

A welcome contrast in our trip came when we moved on southward into the California redwoods. By now, everyone knows about these wonders, but then we were simply "flabbergasted." We also enjoyed stopping at beaches, marveling at each new find in seashells and sea plants washed ashore. We were ferried over the Golden Gate to San Francisco. Dad said, "In 1908, shortly after the earthquake, I saw this city in ruins. Now there was no sign of the quake."

We continued on toward El Segundo, where we spent some time with another former McComb family. I was no longer writing a diary, but Dad comments on the missions and his admiration of suntanned people, especially girls. He says they would "give another angle to Greeley's go west, young man, go west."

Our fifty-cent box of grapes and five-cents-a-dozen oranges were most enjoyable as we crossed the desert toward the Grand Canyon. Again, we were "flabbergasted" by a wonder of nature. Dad announced that he was going to walk down the Kaibab Trail. He claims he warned us, but Mom and I insisted on joining him on the seven-mile trail to the bottom. Going down wasn't half bad and we enjoyed refreshing ourselves in the cold water, exploring a bit, and having lunch.

Going back up was the most difficult work any of us had ever experienced. The seesaw turns seemed endless. We kept saying that surely around the next bend we'd find the bottle of water and the oranges Dad had cached on the way down. It was never soon enough! We had to stop and rest frequently. I remember saying that a flattened rock felt softer than an over-stuffed davenport. Mom and I limped for days. My toenails blackened and came off.

Back home, I went back to school. Not until the third six-weeks report card did my grade in arithmetic show recovery. I had missed about six weeks while my classmates were studying geography of the Western states!

How ironic that this wonder-filled year should have come just before the year that brought so many changes! Have there ever been a father and daughter who had more rewarding times together? My gift was daylong closeness for weeks, but even my younger sisters had an advantage not given to children whose fathers have a job away from home.

Daddy didn't go to Sunday school with us except on Children's Day when his brood participated in "speaking pieces"—dialogues, skits, and songs—as we wore our brand-new dotted Swiss dresses and patent leather shoes. He had no objection to Mama's devotion to the church nor to her requiring us girls to say prayers before climbing into bed each night. But I sensed that Daddy's religion had more to do with Mother Nature than with standard religious dogma. I wish I could remember what books he read, but the only one I do recall is Walt Whitman's *Leaves of Grass*.

Our dad was always pleasant enough when we girls were able to tag him around the farm, but he was usually too busy to pay much attention to us. He gave us a few chores, like taking Laddie to the farthest field to bring in the cows at milking time. At corn planting time, we tagged along barefoot behind a horse-pulled machine that first plowed open a deep, narrow furrow and then periodically dropped in several grains of corn. A device was supposed to cover them, but in uneven or bumpy soil, it sometimes failed. We girls took turns covering them, five for a penny! Later, as green shoots began to grow, a cultivator scratched out weeds between the rows. Then, if soil happened to cover a few plants, we'd rescue them, again five for a penny.

Only once do Irene and I remember Dad spanking us; Mom was in charge of discipline. On that notable occasion, our misdemeanor damaged a stack of materials used to make honeycombs. The equipment had been set up in an upstairs bedroom. A mechanical machine would fold wooden pieces together into small square boxes, insert sticky pieces, and then clamp it all together. This would go into hives, where bees would add honey to those sticky squares. Alas, Irene and I took a fancy to the transparent sheets of paper that would have kept the sticky squares from sticking together if we hadn't removed them!

Though Daddy had a rather sober face, he had amusing nicknames for us and joked with us around the supper table, as he made sure we always cleaned our plates. Irene fondly remembers his squeezing her hand and saying, "cold as ice and twice as nice." In the few pictures we have of him, even the one in which he and his bride are being congratulated by the minister, he looks more thoughtful than expressive. He was slim, sturdy, always clean-shaven, and about a foot taller than his bride. The first thing he did when he came in for supper was to give her a long kiss.

We all remember him sitting by the range in the evening, reading and eating popcorn, his stocking feet on the open oven door if it was cold out. Alyce, who was only five when he left us, says her one memory of him is watching him lace or unlace his long boots with hooks as well as holes.

I wonder what he'd have been like with adolescent daughters. I have a dim memory of his gently chastising mama for powdering our scuffed knees before Sunday school. Would he have hurt Mom and Irene by approving my joining the Unitarian Church, or even going with me as did two of my sisters? Would he and I have agreed about politics and environmental issues but argued about gun control?

## SCHOOL DAYS

My first year of school was the last year for little one-room schoolhouses like Sharpstreet for me. From then on, I went to a twelve-grade consolidated building in McComb. Sharpstreet was not on a street. It was on a narrow country road like the others nearby, including the one in front of my home a mile or so away. The school must have been named for a founder.

Another five-year-old girl, Treva Eiseman, lived right across the road from Sharpstreet. She wanted to go to school with her two brothers. To give her company as a first-grader, I was recruited to join her. It was decided that on Mondays I would walk from home with Loren and Stanley Ewing and walk home with them on Fridays. The large Ewing family, which lived right across the road, were close friends. During the week, I would live at Grandma Smith's and go to school with Aunt Naomi. She was a sixth-grader.

Being with Naomi that year was a blessing for me. Both then and in years to come, she was a greatly admired role model for my sisters and me. She answered our growing-up questions and taught us how to act and how to dress. To get me ready for school that year, she battled a persistent cowlick in my unruly hair. When I visited her not long ago in a retirement home in Florida, it amused her to see that the cowlick was still there. When Hurricane Charley hit Port Charlotte in 2004, she was stranded on the top floor for weeks without electricity or water. A piece of the roof had come through the window into her bedroom.

Elevators couldn't work. When phone service was restored, I learned that she did have drinking water and that one meal a day was walked up the stairs to residents, along with one bucket of water a day to flush the toilet. I suggested that, since she couldn't read or watch TV or use her sewing machine, she might have enough window-light to write an account of the experience. She did and sent it to me for typing and making copies. These made such a hit with family and friends that she continued by writing stories about her life, filled with a unique variety of experiences, including several other encounters with water going astray, mostly floods. At ninety-seven, she still uses fine handwriting to answer letters from her many nieces.

Sharpstreet was a one-room redbrick building with narrow windows and a bell on top. There was no electricity, but it had a coal-fired stove and outdoor toilets. Our teacher, Mrs. Grubb, presided over seventeen pupils in eight grades. In front of the seats, there was the recitation bench. Treva and I sat directly behind it so we could listen in when the teacher called out "fifth grade" or whatever and those pupils came up for their lesson. I must have learned to read by the phonetic method because I remember being confused by the word "sugar." I was puzzled by why that little thieving squirrel would have been fond of a "cigar."

Games at noon and during recess were always a delight. Baseball was the most popular game in the summer. In the winter, we could slide on a depressed area in the yard that was covered with ice. To call us in, whoever asked first got permission to pull the rope to ring the big bell atop the roof.

What a privilege it would be to ring that bell, I thought. I tried and tried to remember to ask first. At last, I succeeded. I could hardly wait for the noon hour to end so I could pull that rope and call everybody in. At last, Mrs. Grubb said, "Now it's time, Carol." I eagerly grabbed the rope and pulled with all my might. My feet were off the floor. I bounced and bounced, but nothing happened. A humiliating lesson: wait until you are qualified for the job! One time I earned a punishment. Mrs. Grubb said I must "stay in" after school. Smugly, I said, "Oh, no! It's Friday and I have to walk home with Loren and Stanley." "Oh, that's all right," she answered. "They have to stay in too."

For the next eleven years, my sisters joined me one by one in scrambling to get ready for the school bus to go to the new community school, which seemed huge at first. All twelve grades, one or two rooms each, were in that one building. Many community-wide activities took place in the large auditorium with a balcony. Farmers' organizations like the Grange held programs, and there were plays and music recitals. Traveling companies like Chautauqua brought educational programs and the music that was probably responsible for my father's admiration for the accordion, a liking he passed along to me. When large doors behind the stage were pulled aside, we could watch competitive basketball games. We students enjoyed going to basketball and football games in surrounding towns.

I enjoyed school and did well. I have a certificate that says I scored fifth in Hancock County in a test given by the state of Ohio. And in a high school spelling bee, my sister Irene and I spelled down the whole high school. After she went down on "chamois," I continued until I was finally tricked with the simple word "plow." I spelled it "plough." I was sure I had read that spelling, but it was deemed wrong.

In the lower grades, however, there were some less "boast-able" memories. I had to stay in from recess in the third grade to work on my multiplication tables. Once I had to "stand on the floor" in front of the room, probably for illegal talking. In high school, I took books home every night, intending to study, but I never did. Instead, I did assignments in study hall when I wasn't reading library books. I liked something written by Leo Tolstoy so much that I became absorbed in reading all I could about him.

All twelve grades went to regular assemblies. There were occasional guest speakers. We younger ones couldn't make sense of the locally famous Dr. Herbert's lectures. By the time I was in high school, however, we had moved to town. On the mile-long walk home, I would stop by his tiny house, where he lived alone surrounded by books. He would willingly lend his books to any of us. There was never the slightest hint of concern about our being alone with him.

We didn't have a school paper, so I started one. It was a pitiful typed affair named *Hi Times*. Several students wrote articles and some drew cartoons. Dick Culp's father had a mimeograph machine in his basement where we could run them off after school. I still laugh at the only copy I saved.

Noontimes were enjoyable, nothing organized. We'd just gad around in the halls and visit. My close friends, Mildred and Bonnie, and I spent time in front of the rest room mirror working on our spit curls. We must have wanted to be attractive to boys, but social life in high school then was much tamer than nowadays. With a rumored exception or two, the extent of our relations with boys, at least for me, consisted of holding hands or an occasional kiss. We enjoyed ourselves in group doings and during daytime football games at home and nighttime basketball games at other county schools.

I acted in two high school plays and in a community play. One night, George Walker took me home from play practice. He had been the lead in a rather romantic part with Nola. On the way home, he mentioned subtly that he wished he could have been opposite someone more inspiring. Shortly after walking me to the door, he drove back to tell me that George Stout and Carlton Strouse had laughingly sprung up from where they had been hiding on the floor of his car's back seat. They joked with him about his "inspiration" and the next day at school teased us even more. I guess that was the closest I came to a high school boyfriend, though it was a purely platonic relationship. Once we went together to a scientific display in North Baltimore.

I don't remember the occasion when my friend Bonnie introduced me to her cousin Donald (not his real name), my first real boyfriend. I was a junior at the time, and he was a junior in college. We wrote letters back and forth for years. He lived in Findlay some ten miles away, but his college was farther away. When he was home, we'd go to movies. I enjoyed a very special dance in Findlay for which I bought a beautiful long, black, form-fitting dress. I've never stopped feeling pain when I recall the moment years later when I said I wanted us to be just friends. That hadn't been on his mind when he drove fifty miles to Toledo to be with me. I had more in common with him, perhaps, than with John, whom I married, but the magic just wasn't there. He became a college professor. Much later, when I shared a space with another high school teacher, my eye caught a textbook on his desk. It was by [Donald Morris] and entitled *Industrial Sociology*.

I was fortunate to have a scholarship that allowed me to attend Bluffton College, a creation of Mennonites, who are like Quakers in their pacifism. I had begun thinking about this most baffling of human problems, how to prevent war and other violent conflict, when I was in the sixth grade. I was assigned an article in our Weekly Reader to report to the class. Having heard much adult conversation about the terrible First World War, I was pleased to learn that sixty-three nations had signed the Kellogg-Briand Peace Pact, in which they agreed to give up war as an instrument of national policy. It is ironic that, in a few years, it would turn out that national leaders were as naïve as that ten-year-old girl!

Since then, non-violent resolution of conflict has been a major concern for me. While World War II was brewing, I was in high school and Leo Tolstoy, author of *War and Peace*, was becoming my hero. With other young people, I participated for years in a Prince of Peace contest sponsored by Ohio churches. Speeches on war and its causes were composed by college students and put into a booklet for high schoolers to memorize and deliver to their congregations. The speaker judged to have done the best job was awarded a bronze medal with the opportunity to compete in the county contest for a silver medal. That winner tried for a gold one at the regional level, then on to the state level in Columbus.

After collecting several bronze medals and a silver one, I finally delivered my speech in Columbus. Though not a winner there, I was offered a two-year scholarship at Bluffton. As my family was still short of money in 1935, that was great luck. I was given a job in the kitchen to pay for my dorm room. I had a joyful two years there.

The challenging courses were not beyond my ability, with the possible exception of biology. Slides in a microscope were hard for me to deal with. I couldn't see what I was supposed to see. I made only Bs there. Nevertheless, I qualified for the Pi Delta group. In "Contemporary Civilization," we had many long pages to read in two multi-volume books in the library. Though these assignments were difficult, they helped me learn to read complex material quickly.

It was this increase in reading ability and in world affairs that led me to continue reading things that would otherwise have been too demanding. In busy years to come, before I finished college, I collected books with ideas about the causes of violent conflict and ways to prevent it. One example is *A Plan for Peace* by Grenville Clark, published in 1950.

I learned enough French to read, but not enough for conversation, as I found years later in France and in Quebec. I enjoyed writing, being on a debate team, and singing in Handel's Messiah with the noted *a capella* choir. Every Christmas, people joined the singing. Mennonites greatly value music. There were concerts. I found their hymns more beautiful than those back home. I played minor parts in a Shakespeare play each year.

We had a rich social life. Freshman girls on the top floor of the dorm became great friends. It was jolly working in the kitchen of the dorm, where I dried glasses and silverware, helped the cook, and set the table. Everyone dressed for dinner. Conversation around tables of twelve was lively. Sometimes, one table would yell out, "We want Bill!" or, "We want Carol!" Either Bill would play the piano or a guy would go upstairs with me to get my accordion.

Dates were quite innocent compared with nowadays. Once, I counted on one hand the times I'd been kissed. Evenings in the library, a boy might ask to walk me home, just off campus if he wanted to smoke. Other times, we would walk to Hankishes in town for a sundae. There was no dancing. We had skating parties in the gym. We had to check into the dorm by 10:00.

A boyfriend was editor of the annual and the *Witmarsum*, our school paper. Our dates were often spent proofreading the paper where it was printed at Bluffton's newspaper offices.

Religion at this Mennonite school and the local church seemed no different from what I had been accustomed to, but I must have begun to think about religion during a class called "Ethics." There was an assignment in which I wrote something to the effect that I thought heaven and hell were right here on earth. This idea was not well received by the professor, as I remember, and may have had something to do with my willingness to make do with two years of college and then go to Toledo. My scholarship was for only two years anyway.

A major advantage of Bluffton was that it was only eighteen miles from home. Mother frequently came and got me so that I could join my sisters and be treated to my favorite dinner, her delicious chop suey. She would take me to Lima to shop for clothes. These were not plentiful, but they were of fine quality and style.

I had started playing my accordion during high school. During weekends and in summer I took a few lessons, first in Findlay and then in Toledo when we heard of Trick Bros., a large accordion store with several teachers. For a while, we went there twice a month. Mother and Eleanor's mother took turns driving the fifty miles. She and I had our lessons with a handsome, dark-haired, accomplished player named John Straubinger.

In the second summer, I went to stay in Toledo with Aunt Thelma. When I got a job as a waitress, I practiced carrying four of Aunt Thelma's plates at a time. It was difficult to keep in mind a long changing list of tasks and determine whether this task or that one should have priority. Tasks included handing out menus, bringing water, answering questions, taking orders and calling them to the chef, being interrupted to serve meals or write bills, and on and on. Most people ordered the "Shoppers Special" at noon: twenty-five cents plus one cent tax. In the evening, thirty-five cents plus one cent tax bought a complete meal; Fifty cents plus two cents included dessert; the "seventy-five-center" customer got special attention indeed!

If I finished early, I could get to the Granada Theater before the sixteen-cent price became twenty-six cents. There was always a double-feature movie. Going home was no problem; street cars were available everywhere and often. That made it easy to spend all my free time at the Trick Bros. accordion store and school. I don't remember how many days I was a waitress instead of an aspiring musician. Nor do I remember when I first became an accordion teacher as well as a student, nor how John and I progressed from being colleagues to becoming close friends.

# RAPID CHANGES

However it came about, I now had a different role in a third kind of school. First I was a student in a public school, then a student in a private college, and now I was one of five teachers at Trick Bros., a commercial school.

My first accordion students had bought our ten-week trial course. This bargain included rental for a twelve-bass instrument for beginners. It was expected that they would progress so rapidly and enjoyably that they would soon become prospects for the full-size 120-bass accordion. Our elder teacher, Sid Dawson, created ten lessons that started with easy, catchy tunes. Each sheet had new skills, helpful hints, and amusing comments, with a new sheet for each lesson. In frequent teachers' meetings, we made changes according to how well the lessons worked with our students.

John taught advanced players, mostly from music arranged and published by Anthony Galla-Rini, the country's top classical and semi-classical accordionist. He spent weeks with us from time to time, inspiring both teachers and students with his playing. With Sid, he helped us with teaching techniques and ways to improve the trial course. He went with us to delicious Italian spaghetti dinners at the Mannones' home. Their daughter Catherine was one of John's students. A bus full of teachers and students went with him for a week at the Interlochen Music Camp in Michigan.

Decades later, sometime in the 90s, I learned that Tony and his wife had moved to California, only thirty miles from where I now live. Members of a local accordion club were delighted when Tony was persuaded to come to La Mesa for a program. So many years had passed since Tony and I had seen each other that we had a lot of catching up to do. I drove to his home in San Marcos to spend a day with him and his wife, sharing any news we had about the Trick Bros. people. Though he was in his late eighties, he was still conducting yearly seminars for accordion players.

In contrast with European and Russian music lovers, the accordion has a poor reputation with many Americans. Tony had contempt for Lawrence Welk. He said his type of music had defined the accordion down for lovers of classical or concert music. In Russia, however, the accordion is used in symphony orchestras. The accordion club of East County arranged concerts by amazingly proficient players from Europe. I bought a CD from one Polish musician, in which he plays Bach, Scarlatti, and Handel pieces. It occurred to me that Toledo's large Polish-immigrant population must have brought a cultural affinity for the accordion, for many of our students were of Polish descent. They invited us to wedding celebrations where we danced to their lively polkas.

Though popular music is much more often played with the guitar, standard songs like Gershwin's fit well with the accordion, where one can play melody with the right hand, bass on the left, and vary dynamics with the bellows. John arranged popular music for our Trick Bros. trio: Eddie Urban, Billy Lengel, and John. He also made arrangements for our student band. The *Toledo Blade* ran a picture of this band in uniform standing in front of more than a hundred additional students who came for a festival from our branch studios in a dozen surrounding towns in Ohio and Michigan.

Trick Bros. teachers and better students played for fifteen minutes every Sunday on radio station WSPD. John and I usually played the theme song, "Caprice Viennois" by Fritz Kreisler. To join us on the program was an incentive for many students.

John's mother doted on him, the youngest of three sons. She made a scrapbook with newspaper clippings of John with Jerry, a violinist. This popular "Johnny and Jerry" team had played nightly in a Washington, DC hotel café. The scrapbook includes a program of an anniversary celebration in an Alexandria, Virginia, hotel featuring "Johnny and Jerry." In contrast, John and a baritone soloist were featured in the program for a concert of classics by the Philharmonic Orchestra back in Toledo.

John used his mother's Packard to take a few of us to the harmony classes our boss, Al Trick, had recommended. I told Al my ten dollars a week didn't allow for the fee, so he gave me a dollar raise. The class didn't do much to make me a better teacher, but I did like riding there with John. Riding horses was even more delightful. I joined him and fellow teacher Jane in taking the riding class of a small Irish jockey, another Johnny, who had a remarkably profane vocabulary. Once I fell off and my friend John came galloping to rescue me from the soft dirt where I landed. No harm except for persistent dusty residue—and words from the other Johnny.

Because our students came for their lessons in after-school hours, it was dark when we finished, so John started driving me home. We went together to various functions and finally on real dates. At first, it was double dates, movies with his friends Bill and Maxine. Then on Sundays he would often take me along to Bill Bonser's home for long visits. Bill would soon be an MD; Doc Bonser was an eye specialist; Bill's mother Alice grew gorgeous begonias in their long adjacent greenhouse. Sometimes I browsed the family's extensive library.

Other Sundays, I went along with John and his parents for long rides in the country. His father, totally deaf, spun dreams of moving to the country and growing a garden when he retired. Amazingly, this was a dream that was to come true! One fourth of July, we drove close to fireworks so he could hear the booms.

We went to movies on other Sundays or holidays, but John would unkindly keep me in suspense about when that would be. I would wait for his phone call there at Flower-Esther. This place with the fancy name was a home for working girls sponsored by the Methodist Church. For three dollars a week, I rented a tiny room about double the width of a bed, long enough for a chest, and with a nice wide window. There was one bathroom for every seven girls. We could get breakfast for fifteen cents. It wasn't far from the store by streetcar, but once in a while we would share a cab.

Johnny kept me in suspense again when in the movies I would

wonder when he would reach over to hold my hand. Our relationship moved faster than it seemed at the time. I had moved to Toledo in the summer of 1937. By late summer in 1938, we were making wedding plans. I had fantasies of a light housekeeping flat, and we started saving money in a joint account. There were dinners at his home with his father and mother. Myrtle let me help her in the kitchen and learn the secrets of a good cook.

She offered the Packard for a honeymoon if we would wait for snow to let up. On April 16, we were married in a simple wedding in the McComb church where my father's funeral had been held. My sister Mary Lou was my only attendant. John's close friend, John Saalfield, a successful businessman, was his best man. Two cousins ushered. We received greetings at the door when guests departed. There was a dinner for family around Mother's extended round oak table. We left for Kentucky and other Southern states.

For over a year, we lived in a room at the home of John's parents. I continued teaching until I became too pregnant. Then I set up a desk upstairs in our bedroom where I copied sheet music using a mimeograph machine with lighted frame and stencils. Our baby girl was born in the middle of the night. In those days, we spent a much longer time in the hospital. My roommate and I liked comparing our babies and ideas about how to care for them. We compared experiences and ideas with Bill and Maxine whose Mary Alice was born shortly before our Judy. Bill was a doctor.

Mom Straubinger was beside herself with pleasure when we returned from the hospital. She bought a Bathinette. The lid on top was a platform for changing diapers and dressing the baby. When lifted up and dropped behind, it exposed the tub. I don't think plastics were used at that time, so it was probably made of rubber. Mom greatly enjoyed helping with the daily ritual and in many other ways. Dad chuckled gleefully when he watched Judy. It had been many years since the folks had been that close to a baby, except when John's brother and his wife from Annapolis brought their first grandson for a brief visit.

Both Mom and Dad accepted me completely. As parents of three sons, they treated me as if I was now their daughter. I learned to care about nutrition as I helped Mom in the kitchen, cleaning lots of green vegetables and hearing her quote her favorite expert, Victor Lindlahr.

Women from the League for the Hard of Hearing were frequent luncheon visitors. Dad's total deafness, of course, was responsible for Mom's activity in this organization. I was amazed to see how well these women could communicate with lip reading. I didn't notice any sign language.

When Judy was about four months old, the Tony Mannone family bought a big old house to remodel, live in, and create apartments to rent. The attic was lit by dormer windows and a skylight. It had a bedroom big enough for a crib, a good-sized kitchen, and a miniature bathroom. The laughingly named living room was down a flight of stairs on the second floor. It had a large window looking out to a deck, but it had only enough space for a love seat, a side chair, and our wedding-gift coffee table. We bought our first piece of fine furniture, a beautiful green-and-white-linen love seat.

A door at the foot of the stairs led to the deck overlooking a park. When John Saalfield and his wife came to visit, we hauled chairs down from the kitchen and sat out on the deck. If I wanted to take advantage of the park, someone had to haul Judy's buggy down two flights of stairs.

Money we had saved was enough for a gas stove and a refrigerator. We painted a used table and chairs. Our used bed looked fine with a tufted light brown bedspread, a wedding gift. We loved the linoleum on the kitchen floor. Tony had laid it with a delightful variety of colorful scrap pieces in different sizes and designs. Charlie Capron, a family friend who dealt in antiques and discards from large estates, gave us a beautiful chocolate-brown-bordered strip of carpet, which had graced someone's wide staircase.

Mom Straubinger was unhappy to see us move. She felt that her hospitality had been rejected. She adored Judy and had been kind to us. It was hard for her to be realistic as she saw our enthusiasm for the change.

# FIRST HOME

We now had a major drawback: with no car to use, John had to take a bus to work. I shopped for groceries with Anna Mannone. I experimented with new recipes, like the ones I had tried out on my sisters when Mother was away working. They still laugh about burying my cherry fritters, one of my unsuccessful experiments.

Here I wasn't quite sure what to cook on Sundays, for Anna would often come up in the afternoon with a big bowl of Tony's wonderful Italian spaghetti and meat balls. Delicious aromas from the sauce he simmered for hours in the basement wafted up to our attic apartment. Nothing I cook has ever smelled so good.

I did laundry in the basement and hung it on clotheslines on a wide deck off the second floor. It was there that I chatted with a woman from the other apartment and learned about new houses being built after passage of the FHA, the Federal Housing Administration. She gave me an ad telling all about some tiny houses that could be bought with $400 down and only a little more a month than the twenty-five dollars we paid for rent. My mental wheels now in rapid motion, I began trying to persuade John that we could manage this drastic undertaking. One compelling reason was that Judy, now walking, had to spend so much time in her playpen under the skylight.

When John agreed, I borrowed $400 from my mother, applied for the loan, and got it. We soon moved into this new sparkling wonder, a home of our own on 323 Pasadena Blvd. It was smaller than most apartments, but there were two bedrooms and various features that were revolutionary for 1941. We soon learned that companies making building equipment were eager to cash in on the fact that the FHA produced so many people who were now able to afford a house.

Frank Hawkins of Libby-Owens-Ford, one of these companies, came to see us shortly after we moved in. We were the only buyers of the ten demonstration models that had any children, and they wanted to start an advertising campaign with an article and ads in *Parents* magazine. There would be pictures and an article under my name. I balked: our only furniture was the love seat and coffee table, unless you count the two luscious strips of carpet sewn together and fitting perfectly on the living room floor, 11' 4 ½" by 16' 2", figures etched permanently in my memory.

"Well," said Frank, "I'll see what the company thinks about that problem." He came back in a day or two with an offer to give us $100 to buy enough furniture to improve the picture. However, I said, "You'll never believe this, Mr. Hawkins, seeing how poor we look, but we are perfectly willing to make do with leftovers and empty spaces until we can afford to buy just what we like. When I shopped at LaSalle and Koch's for draperies and looked around at their furniture, I saw nothing but old-fashioned eighteenth-century reproductions. I want to wait until they start showing what we like, the nice clean lines of Danish modern chairs I've seen in magazines."

Whatever Frank may have thought of such lunacy, he consulted once more with the "powers that be" and came back with this plan: he'd been wanting to visit relatives in Michigan anyway, so I could ride up with him and his wife, stay with them overnight, and then go to one of the many Grand Rapids furniture stores, the Widdicomb factory where they produce fine modern furniture. At wholesale prices I could buy as much as I wanted on my own in addition to what they had allotted.

I couldn't afford to buy many extras, but I did end up with a nicely furnished living room. I would go outside and look through the windows and admire it. The larger chairs were made with colorful fabrics I selected. There were two dining chairs, cushioned chairs with plainer fabric, wicker backs, and graceful walnut frames. There were two end tables and two modern lamps. It was all delivered promptly, perhaps with urging from the companies who were eager to start their advertising campaign and make a movie to show builders their newfangled products.

An ad listed nine companies. Libby-Owens-Ford, the glass company in Toledo, was most prominent. *Parents* magazine mentioned a "wing-mirrored medicine cabinet ... triple mirrors on closet doors ... Vitrolite structural glass above the bathtub ... impervious to splashing." All the bathroom fixtures were light-blue Briggs Beautyware. "In homes costing many times as much, you will not find bathrooms more beautiful." Houses down the street that had been built the previous year had basements with coal-burning furnaces. Ours had Janitrol fully automatic blower-type gas heaters in the attic. Though the previous year's houses down the street had conventional windows, we had large Andersen horizontal sliding windows.

In the end, we felt like the luckiest people in the world except for the fact that John hadn't been able to join in the fun of bringing it all about. He was now working two jobs. Because of WW II, he had been obligated to join the defense effort by taking a job at a Jeep factory. Not wanting to abandon his accordion students, he took the bus directly from Trick Bros. downtown to the factory nearby four days a week. He worked the swing shift and then walked home unless he got a ride with a fellow worker.

Money was now more plentiful, but we used the extra for war bonds. I wanted to make every penny count, so I kept an exact count of expenditures. I still have the record. One item says, "Got weighed .01." Wartime rationing was no problem. I didn't even use all my sugar stamps now that I was following nutritional advice. A grocery store was only two blocks away. I didn't mind the lack of a car. I read a lot and got acquainted with neighbors. For a while, a sewing club met at my house. I had the only treadle sewing machine on the block. If there were electric machines, none of us had one.

Luckily, Mom Straubinger was available for emergencies. That became especially lucky when we learned that we were going to have another child. Our lifestyle was about to change dramatically, and we would need her. At least we had a few months to get settled and to make plans for Judy's new sister or brother. It's hard to believe, but our benighted plans didn't take into account the fact that Dr. Miller and the hospital were fifty miles away in McComb. Perhaps we had kept the car in our garage when the time was near instead of having to call Mom Straubinger.

We made the trip in time, however, on August 26, 1941. The tiny hospital was the current incarnation of a building at Ingold Park that had originally been the high school for McComb's 1100 inhabitants. Then when high school became part of the new consolidated school, a swimming pool appeared and the building was used for changing clothes and for a small library. Now it was Doc Miller's headquarters—an operating room, a wee nursery, and one room for patients. My memory doesn't yield anything about prenatal care visits to the doctor.

I kept saying I was going to have twins, but everyone else was surprised when a 6 lb., 5 oz. girl was followed by a 5 lb., 3 oz. boy! All went well. I was told that John had fainted, but this was probably an exaggeration. Mother was thrilled, but Grandma Smith said, "Oh, the poor girl!" News spread fast. I was besieged by relatives and high school friends. Suggestions for names were plentiful. As Jack is a diminutive for John and I liked Jill for a girl, that combination was briefly considered, but we rejected it as too cute. I thought of Peter and Paula, but we settled on David and Donna.

When I first laid eyes on the twins as they were placed by my side in the delivery room, they appeared exactly as I've seen them all their lives. Donna was plump and placid; David was wiry and energetic. That has never changed.

Sadly, there was a tragedy to dampen the scene. My roommate Gaynelle had her baby the next day. All that night, we could hear unusual cries from the nursery, and the next day her baby died. Imagine the situation! Here I was being congratulated for my two; she had none. It's too bad she couldn't have been moved to a different room.

When our expanded family went back to Toledo, my sister Irene soon came to us from Kentucky, where she had been working in a sort of clinic. She was a godsend in many ways. First, we had to deal with sleeping arrangements. The parents' bed was moved to Judy's smaller bedroom; her crib came to the larger room along with bunks. Irene slept in the upper bed; two makeshift cribs occupied the lower one.

Irene's help was indispensable. There were bottles to prepare, babies to feed every three hours or so, and diapers to wash in the Bendix washer and hang on lines outside. When winter came, they would freeze solid before drying. David developed pyloric spasms. This is a problem with the stomach that causes projectile vomiting. We would feed him very slowly and carefully as the doctor ordered, but almost invariably, the formula would end up across the room. We tried less milk more often. We tried thickening it with pablum with only limited success. It looked as if surgery would be required. Finally, the doctor prescribed a medication, probably a sedative, to mix into a small bottle half an hour before the formula. It worked and David began to gain a little weight. My mother was distressed that he was so much smaller than his sister. She thought we should try feeding him more.

Would John find it impossible to sleep when he came home in the morning? No, his two jobs tired him enough to make him impervious to the inevitable racket, but Judy would tell the babies, "Don't cry. Daddy's sleeping."

Irene wrote down daily notes about progress and fun. One bit tells of her routine for cleaning the kitchen floor. Paste wax was used for finishing the job instead of the liquid form available later on. The floor had to be polished by hand. Irene would put Judy on a big Turkish towel and pull that weighted polisher around the kitchen to the tune of much laughter. Her diary is full of quotations, first Judy's and then the twins'.

Here are some samples from Irene's diary: 9/10: "Judy always says thank you now. Ask her how her sore mouth is: All right, thank you. Is her soup too hot? Just right, thank you." 3/21: "David has had no use for the teeter-babe till now, but today he put on a look of resignation and made some businesslike bounces as if we'd never be satisfied until he showed some appreciation."

We had many visitors on Sundays. Family members and friends showered us with useful and delightful clothes and toys. There was always an entertaining new development about the children to share in addition to discussing the outside world.

One gift was a little red wagon. Someone gave Judy a tricycle for her third birthday. We had put two boxes in the wagon so the twins could ride along to the grocery store. Now Judy could pull the wagon with her tricycle. The whole family was thrilled with my Christmas gift from Mom Straubinger, a piano.

Amazingly, when new playmates moved right across the street, it happened that they too were twins, Jerry and Joyce! They were older than David and Donna, but not as old as Judy.

While Irene was with us, I took Judy along and went to McComb by bus for a few days to see my mother. She had sold her house and was now living with Grandma Smith on Main Street. My youngest sister Alyce and her little daughter Vicky were with her. Another time, I made a sad trip when Grandma died of appendicitis before either sulfa drugs or penicillin was used. I didn't want to view the body in the parlor, but Mama insisted. I would have preferred to remember Grandma alive.

Irene took a few courses at Toledo U. When the twins were about two, it was time for her to move on. She had made it possible to get our life in good order. That was a great blessing and more than enough. She finished college, got her MA degree in Michigan, and then moved to Israel as an evangelical Christian.

My religious ideas were not like hers, but I had let her take Judy along to her Sunday school a few times. By now, the children were potty trained, so it was possible to take them along with me when I discovered Toledo's Unitarian church. For sixty-five cents, we could take a taxi there. John wasn't interested in going, and he needed time to rest after his exhausting week.

The exhaustion finally took a toll on his endurance. Over breakfast one morning, we made a plan to do something about it. From time to time, John had reminisced about the two high school years he had spent in San Diego. He, his brother Phil, and their mother had been persuaded by John's aunt Jim to see whether living in a sunny climate would help Phil's asthma. She paid rent for an apartment in San Diego so they could try it for a year or two. Dad stayed alone on his job back in Toledo.

Phil stayed in San Diego. He worked for Standard Iron and then married Ruby, the boss's daughter. Both John and his parents dreamed of joining Phil someday. That day came the morning when the conversation went something like this: John said, "Let's move to California." I answered, "OK." Of course, there was then the question of a job. A few letters back and forth ensued. Then Phil's boss offered John work with Standard Iron, which was fortunately a defense-related firm.

First, we would sell our house. Much as we loved it, it was now too small. John would go to San Diego, start the job, and buy a house. The children and I would live with Mama until there was a place for us. Until then, we arranged storage for any furniture we didn't sell or give away.

Not knowing how long it would take to sell the house, I put an ad in the paper right away with a price of $5995. John felt that was too nervy; we had paid only $4250. I said, "Oh, we are in no hurry. We can come down later if necessary." When the ad appeared in the morning paper, a couple bought our house before breakfast even though they couldn't have immediate possession.

# WESTWARD HO! (1944)

Now it was time to decide what to save and what to get rid of. It didn't make sense to pay for moving the heaviest items that could be replaced. First we gave the slide and the swing set to Cousin Evelyn for her children. We'd sell the gas stove and refrigerator. The new owners of the house bought the refrigerator. The wartime economy was responsible for the unique way we "sold" the stove. One of the strange economic conditions was the fact that most unrationed items became scarce or unobtainable, whereas expensive luxuries were readily available. For example, John couldn't find a cheap cotton shirt, though the store did have silk shirts. Well laid plans might go astray. For instance, I had just saved enough Betty Crocker coupons for a set of everyday silverware. Alas, it was too late. When I sent the coupons in as directed, I got back the obvious reply: "Due to wartime needs …" But it so happened that an acquaintance who was in the business of selling sterling silver needed a gas stove. Voila! We penny pinchers now owned a set of beautiful silver in the William and Mary pattern we chose.

When the moving company came to pick up the items we would need in California, I was engaged in wrapping breakables in towels and clothing. "Oh, don't bother with that," they said. We're professionals: we can do that better than you can." (Ha!) They would store everything until we were settled.

Before John left, we talked about our potential new home. It was understood that his parents would eventually be joining us. Dad would retire before long, and he was eager to embark on his long-held dream of building a house and growing a garden. We also needed to consider location. We shouldn't be too far inland, even though John would have a company car. When we studied a map, I suggested, "What about this 'Elca John'?" He answered, "Oh no. That's way too far and it's a lousy road out there as I recall."

John took a train to Phil's in San Diego. I took the kids and went to live in McComb with Mother until he was ready for us. Needless to say, time couldn't go fast enough for me. Letters flew back and forth. The few months went well enough. I visited high school friends Mildred and Bonnie. The children had a place to play and neighbor children to play with. Mother was working in the post office. My youngest sister Alyce and her daughter Vicky were also staying with Mother while Alyce's husband was in the army.

Meanwhile in San Diego, Phil, Ruby, and Ruby's mother enjoyed helping with the search. To John's surprise, El Cajon looked promising. As home building was not allowed during the war, the owner of a seven-acre grape ranch had obtained permission to add another chicken house to the two he already had. He must have had a different use in mind for this structure, however, for the large picture window and the fine wood in the open-beam ceiling seemed unnecessary for the enjoyment of the average chicken! It would be necessary to add a bathroom, however. We would need to locate fixtures and a plumber.

John sent me a sketch of the floor plan to dream over. In detailed letters to me and his father, he described the seven-acre ranch. Dad offered to lend us the $7400 price. Equity and profit from the Toledo house with cash from our war bonds gave us enough for moving expenses, train fare, and repaying Mother's $400.

The week before we were to leave, I had an unforgettable experience. My friend Mildred was in the McComb hospital. She had just had a baby. On the way to visit her, I walked by the post office to see Mother. She gave me the shocking news. She had just learned that Mildred's husband had been killed in the Normandy invasion. I was not the person to break that awful news to Mildred. It took all the acting power I was capable of to direct my mind away from the tragedy and toward joy over baby Vicky Lynn.

At long last, the time came to move on. It was late December and we had train tickets for departure from a nearby town, Deshler. Mother and Webster took us there in a windy blizzard. Breathlessly, we made it, snowsuits, caps, mittens, galoshes, suitcases, and all. The feeder train would meet the Superchief in Chicago. This shorter leg of the trip was the only trying part of the journey. We weren't able to find a whole row, but did get a seat in front of another. Still, the three year-old youngsters were fearful. The worst problem was the overheated train. All those snowsuits, mittens, etc. had to come off. When one child had to go to the toilet, everyone had to go. There was no way they would stay behind in that scary place. As we neared Chicago, all those caps, mittens, etc, had to be located and put on. We managed to endure that ordeal and the various complications of getting onto the Superchief. Then the hard part was over.

We had the good fortune to be installed in a "roomette." What luxury! It was a perfect setup for the three-day trip. There was a tiny toilet room, a long bench along the inner wall, and a booth with a table and seats for looking out the window. That pleasure, books, and songs compensated for the lack of exercise. A little one-octave wooden xylophone made singing the favorite activity. There's a family joke about that xylophone. It had been given to Donna for Christmas. When she opened the package and held it up vertically for all to see, she said, "Oh, a fence!" Her voice expressed pleasure as if that was always what she had wanted, a fence. We tease Judy about another family joke. Once, when the train got too close to a chasm for her, she ran toward the inner side of the room to balance the weight of the car to prevent the train from falling over.

The open space between cars was so frightening when we headed toward the dining car for our first meal that arrangements were made to bring all our meals to our room. The booth by the window could easily be transformed into a bed. The other bench was wide enough for a bed. After three enjoyable days reading, singing, and surveying by window half a continent, we reached Los Angeles for a joyful reunion. Only two days late for our happy New Year kiss, we were now on our way for a happy new chapter in our lives.

We rode to San Diego to spend a few days in Phil and Ruby's house. The next day after arrival, I did a large washing and hung it outside in the sun to dry. What a contrast! We left Ohio in a blizzard and hung laundry out to dry in the California sun. I've loved it here ever since.

# EL RANCHO

When the moving man delivered our stuff and we bought bunk beds, we were ready to enjoy life in our chicken house. Instead of dredging details from memory, I copy here some excerpts from a year of Round Robin letters. For more than sixty years, we five Poe girls have used these letters to keep in touch with each other and especially with Mother. Alas, though she had five daughters, four of us had scattered about; only Alyce remained near her in Ohio.

Edna was a navy nurse. Mary was in the Women's Army Corp (WAC). Irene moved about and then wound up in Israel. I sent the first letter to Mother and Alyce. They added theirs and sent them on, and the Round Robin started. When all five came back to me, I saved my old one as a diary and wrote a new one. It goes on to this day, with few interruptions.

The following copies describe how I experienced that first year in our El Cajon ranch where I had three main jobs. I ran a preschool for my three tots, started building a subsistence ranch, and served as contractor for an expansion on our two-bedroom house. I see that my letters barely mention this third activity. First, I drew plans for two more bedrooms and a half bath. Also, there was to be a cement porch the full length of the house. I hired a carpenter for $1.50 an hour. He helped me find a plumber, an electrician, and a roofer. Soon John's parents, now called "Nana and Pop," would live here while Pop built their own house.

*January 18, 1945*

Dear Girls,

Oh, what a beautiful morning! The sun shines, birds twitter, and the grass is green. But it's cold getting up in the morning. No use having a furnace fire for just a few hours in the morning and evening; it gets so warm in the daytime that you can go out in a sunsuit if you want to. So, at my first opportunity I'm going to get wooly slippers, a warm robe, and flannel pajamas. Imagine moving to California and stocking up on items such as these! Remember, I left Ohio in a blizzard and three train-days later, I hung clothes to dry outdoors.

It is so cloudy and foggy in the morning you're sure it will rain. Then suddenly you look out and the sky is as blue as a day in June. The hills have a disappearing act too. Now you see them, now you don't. Sometimes they seem close, sometimes far away. Many are within walking distance. I've made some egg salad sandwiches and pretty soon the kids and I are going for a picnic on the lower part of a hill on our own land.

The movers ruined or damaged many of our belongings. The cable on my sewing machine looked as if it had been broken then fixed. The cable was too short to let the top down. The head falls away from the frame when the machine is closed, but wonder of wonders, it still sews. The record player doesn't work. Worst of all, some cups and other saucers from my china collection are smashed. I guess the movers thought that since they didn't match, they weren't important, so they put them in the bottom of a barrel! I'm never going to move again!

Last night, I went to a grocery. With the refrigerator not working and John away with the company car, cooking is a real challenge, not helped by shortages. The grocery had no toilet paper, margarine, cottage cheese, canned meat, etc. What they did have would make a shorter list. Sometimes you can have only one quart of milk. With tragedies happening daily, though, this seems trivial indeed.

The rest of today I am going to spend knocking out loose nails from the packing crates and separating the boards. Maybe we can make something out of them.

*February 6, 1945*

Dear Girls,

No, Mom I am *not* going to write "Dear Girls and the Old Lady." The term girl is hereby to be defined as "a female of any age, actual or admitted." I am taking it to mean us-all. OK? Forgive me for raving about this beautiful spot ... It smells like April outside. We plan to put in a garden soon.

I spoke too soon about the shortages. The store I wrote about last time was Black Diamond. But the Safeway stores here are like A&P back in Ohio, well stocked, considering. They have tiny zucchini, wonderful heads of lettuce for 5 cents each. The enormous oranges are surprisingly expensive, though.

*March 21, 1945*

Dear Mom, Irene, Mary, Edna, Alice,

What a lineup! As I write the names down one by one, I get the feeling a miser must have when he counts his gold pieces. I miss you. Your letters buzz with talk of get-togethers at which I will be absent. Mary and Irene are coming to McComb for a weekend. Edna is coming home this spring. But I asked for it. Sometimes I get a sudden pang and think, "What have I done, moving way out here?" Then I start doing something quick, by way of giving myself a mental anesthetic. It's OK then, almost.

Our pigs are growing. We are going to start chickens next week. I think we'll get fifty to start with. I'm getting enthusiastic about the farming aspect of this venture. I bought a book, *Five Acres and Independence*. I've been working out a crop rotation scheme. How I wish Daddy were still alive; I could ask him all those questions that come up.

*April 12, 1945*

Dear Robins,

Guess what! It's raining! But yesterday and Monday were so beautiful it took my breath away. The sky is a vaster dome out here. Buried in the weeds along the two chicken houses I found some exquisite pink, rose, and lavender sweet peas. Having borrowed a tractor, John is having a great time plowing up everything in sight. He sits up there looking for all the world like a kid with a new tricycle. David becomes hysterical with glee when John lets him ride.

Judy, at five, has graduated from ironing hankies to aprons. She dresses the kids, helps them make beds, and sets the table. When David broke off a strap from his overalls, she said she'd fix it. So I padded a thimble so it would stay on, threaded the needle, knotted the thread, and went back to work. She completed the job. Though I may have seen neater jobs, it did hold and is still holding after three laundries. She learned her letters, though the only help she got from me was answering questions. She is now teaching Donna.

Donna is my best dish wiper. They all help, sometimes all at the same time! It has finally reached the point where they are often a real help. It's worth undergoing the bothersome training period, for they can really help if I let them.

*May 16, 1945*
Dear DEAR Girls,

Gee, your letters really turned the trick this time, and after I'd boasted that I hadn't been crying with homesickness yet. Does anyone know who said "To go away is to die a little"? When you leave home for good, it's as if you are in purgatory or heaven or somewhere, carrying on an existence apart, able to know what is happening to those you left on earth, but unable to make real contact with them … Creepy, eh? But I *will* see you all again or know the reason why. Now don't all start telling me the reason why!

I want to enter a protest. You kids are always saying things that pique my curiosity rather than satisfy it. Mary, for example; you have probably talked for hours about your wedding plans, what Harry says about the European situation, when he's coming, where you'll live, and what he'll do, whether you'll honeymoon in California (!) and what you'll wear. Oh, and will Edna be bridesmaid? I found Harry's picture in *Life* magazine last month. What about his being a flight surgeon? What are they required to do, actually operate during flight, or what?

I have been in the garden almost constantly. The tomatoes are almost ready to blossom, the corn, green beans, and the limas are up, also the chard, carrots, beets, turnips, patty squash, zucchini, cucumbers, and melons. The parsley and the spinach haven't come up yet. A few sweet potato plants came up by themselves, from last year. The bugs, however, have made up their minds to eat the whole works. They will, too, if I let up on my campaign with the squirt gun. And I have to water everything. You know there is no rainfall between April and October.

Our chickens are growing like mad. They eat all the time. We've lost only one of our sixty-five. They should be ready to eat in a couple of months and so will the pig. Are you all having the meat shortage as badly as we are? However, when you read about civilian prisoners in the Philippines having to live on nothing but spinach and rice for two years and others in the world worse off, you realize that we safe-at-home folks are well fed indeed. After all, we can always fill up on popcorn. We do too, almost every day.

The kids, outdoors all the time, are toast-brown. They look funny in the bathtub with their little white bottoms where the sunsuits had been. The other day I caught the twins in an unlawful enterprise; they had put a dozen or so chicks in a big cardboard carton. No harm done; they were sound asleep.

Months ago we did an experiment from the *Children's Activities* magazine. We had put a cold pie pan over rising steam, causing drops of water to condense on it. Well, the other day Judy came in from the hot sun and said, "Mama. When we got the pan hot, drops of water came out and now I'm hot and drops are coming out on me." She may have missed the point of the experiment, but how about that observation, thought process, and memory! She calls the ever-present lightning bugs "underbugs" because she finds them under things.

So many planes fly over that the kids seldom look up, but when a car goes by, they run to watch. They make jeeps and tanks out of pieces of leftover lumber. And I was never going to give them war toys! They have their own hammer and saw. I hear pounding from one chicken coop all day.

*June 6, 1945*

Dears,

Mom, what do you mean by "What do I think about your coming out here this summer"? You know perfectly well that I can hardly wait to show you our farm. Sure, it will be better next year, but think of that wasted time. Tell Webster that I beat him with corn planting. Mine's up already. I put in about a thirtieth of an acre of hog corn. Tell him his fences aren't good enough if the hogs get out. Ours never dream of getting out.... Well, maybe they dream about it, but they never do it. We don't have them on pasture; we just throw a little corn and barley into the pen, some weeds once in awhile, garbage, water.

Did I tell you-all about the pup? Just an ordinary dog, full of mischief and too obstreperous for any good use. The kids renewed their pleading for a dog after Patsy brought hers over and acted so superior about it. So when Bud Winsby gave us this brown midsize mutt we had to accept. The kids immediately named him "Poochy." Same as Patsy's. He barks at me when I make him get out of the garden. When I just bark back, he runs away with his tail between his legs.

Someone asked about the chicken "battery." It costs about $25 and takes about a square yard of floor space. We put it in an all-purpose chicken house. It is very easy to clean. The chicks stand on a wire floor and the droppings fall onto a pullout drawer lined with newspaper. The top deck of this triple-decker has a heater. We put in there thirty day-old chicks that we buy from a hatchery. When they are a month old, half of them are put in each of the lower two decks, then we add another thirty on top. We have thirty tender chickens a month with one yard of space, ten minutes a day, and about 32 cents a pound for feed. *(2008 comment: Judy will be appalled when she reads this. She is emphatically opposed to treating animals cruelly for our own benefit. That's why she is a vegetarian. I see her point.)*

*June 30, 1945*

Dears,

We've been busy buying a cow, a pretty little Guernsey with

her first calf. I read in the paper that we are in the midst of a severe milk shortage in Southern California. Butter will eke out our meager supply of ration points. Now, if I can just remember how to milk!

The kids are getting buggy—jars of beetles and snails all over the house. Donna woke up one night crying that ants were all over her. No wonder.

We took the kids to a circus last Saturday. It looked as if much of it was over their heads, but all week they've recounted and reenacted almost everything they saw. They chuckled and squealed at dogs doing tricks—and at an old-timer act with a kicking donkey, trapeze actors high in the air, tigers jumping through a fire, etc.

*July 26, 1945*
Well, Girls,

We are now in that blistering hot California summer everyone warned me about, but guess what! I'm not suffering. It's 90 now. Recently, it was 95, 102 out by the chicken pens, but there's a fine breeze. We certainly get our money's worth from a bath, though. Perspiration doesn't roll off nor is it ever visible, it just evaporates right away and that's what keeps us cool.

I moved the pullets out to the laying shed. They had better get all set to lay eggs by October. I expect a dozen or two a day. I made cottage cheese this morning. I make several pounds a week. We have superb ice cream from a real freezer, fresh peach, raspberry, etc. We have broiled and fried chicken and sweet corn.

*September 7, 1945*
Dears,

Hi! Look, Mary, a new typewriter ribbon! Now quit scolding. I'm having to get used to not hitting the keys with a hammer. How I envied Mom and Edna the day of your wedding. I suppose all of you will get to meet the new brother before I will. But then, you all haven't met Bessie yet. No offense, Harry. Bessie, you know, is our darling red-and-white jumping cow.

Mom, thanks for the puzzles you sent for the twins' fourth birthday. They got a warm reception. They were just right, not too easy, and not too hard. Thanks too for the rum-flavored post-war bars. I like them better than John's birthday candy, the first box we've seen in ages.

Alyce, David and Donna are now old enough to enjoy the cunning cards you sent. They stuck theirs and Daddy's too around the rim of their mirror.

Edna, congratulations, Registered Nurse! Now that you are free and mistress of your own fate, why not give San Diego a fling? It's a wonderful city—would be even without the sailors. Now get some practice in obstetrics and pediatrics. Then you can come and help me when the triplets come along. Seriously, though, if I ever have another baby, I hope one of you can come and help me because I'd like to try a new theory.

Irene, do you have an MA after your name now? Next it will be a PhD and we'll have to call you Dr. Poe. Just think, in only a week or so, the Poe family will have three titles, RN, MA, and MRS.

You are to be joined by another newsmaker, a five-year-old at this address. Judy starts school tomorrow, an important landmark for me as well as for her! She's agog with anticipation and she acts very grown up whenever she thinks about it. She wears pigtails and red ribbons and has a front tooth out, so she looks just right for her role.

We played school with the kids the other night. They enter into the spirit of make believe so well that when I'm teacher they look at me as if they're seeing me for the first time. Rather disturbing. They all know the "facts of life" now. We had our cow bred the other day. They're all eagerly looking forward to the blessed event.

Lest you think it's all work and no play here in Eden, you must hear about our social life. Sometimes we have people here for chicken dinners or ice cream and cake later in the evening. Last Saturday night, we went to a dance at the Rowing Club with Ruby and Phil. We met scores of their friends. Next week, we join several of them in Ruby's dad's box at a horse show. Mr. Winsby is John's boss. Recently we were his guests at a birthday party in Tijuana, just across the border, my first time in Mexico. With him, his wife Sade, son Bud and his wife, we had a superb dinner. We drank the boss's health in champagne. We had strict orders not to give him a gift—absurd anyway since he's so rich he has everything he could possibly want. I made him a batch of cookies anyway. He was pleased.

John's work is not very exciting. He drives around town in his company car and calls on stores and other businesses selling them hand trucks, bearings, casters, etc. Standard Iron doesn't make these things; they just handle them as a sideline. Introducing himself and selling things is new for John and difficult.

Her teacher says Judy is extremely shy, afraid to talk. However, she likes school a lot and talks plenty about it at home. I know the names of all the kids in her room. At her table are Mary, Steven, David—and Gary Apple. We hear a lot about Gary Apple. One day she rounded up the twins and me to play a game she just learned. You make a circle and the one who's "it" runs around it with a hanky—and so on. The only problem: three don't make much of a circle. Judy was disappointed that she had never been "it" at school. But the next day she reported that she had been the farmer's wife in a game called "Farmer in the Dell." Must be something new. Ha!

I don't think mother love ever reaches such a high point as the day she sees her child leave her protection and go out in the world alone. You pray that everyone will be kind, that she will not be hurt in any way, that none of her enthusiasm will be squelched.

After about two days of school with the accompanying grooming details such as fingernails, Judy proclaimed, "I want to *always* be very neat after this." The lure of mud pies causes some backsliding on this resolution.

David and Donna are excited about school too. They say, "Judy, what did you outline at school today? What did you have for lunch?" They are forever playing school, just like we kids used to do. They always want me to be the teacher. They come in from the yard to color and cut, then I'm to say, "it's recess time," and they will go out to swing again. Then I must say, "Ding Dong," and they will come in again, insisting that I read them a story.

*November 7, 1945*

Dear Family,

John's Mom and Pop are here now. There was quite a bit to do when they arrived. That's why I'm late with the Robin. Sorry.

Something happened. Pooch had been a naughty dog all along, following us no matter how we scolded, running out into the road, standing there like a big, clumsy lummox while cars squealed to a stop.

One time, he followed us to town. We were eager to get to the barbers' where we could close the door on him, expecting he'd get discouraged and go home. Too bad the barber hadn't taken some other day off. The dime stores occurred to us as a refuge. Too bad it was so hot that all the stores left their doors open that day. The strangeness of the new environment didn't make Pooch the least bit bashful. He just walked right in (with a little friend he'd made along the way). I wanted to get a dog collar but I was embarrassed to ask for one for fear the clerks would know it was our dog that was making such a fool of himself.

Well, you can see that such a "no account" dog would come to no good end. Nonetheless, Judy and I were shocked and dismayed when we saw his big brown body, a red pool at his mouth, lying quite still in the middle of Washington Street. We had been puzzled that morning that he was not skulking after us on the way to the bus.

To make a spot on the ground soft enough for grave digging, I had to soak it all morning. It was upsetting to look out the back door and see Pooch stiff and starry-eyed on the wagon with which I'd hauled him all the way from the road. Are you wondering how the kids met this encounter with Death?

Donna: What are we going to do with our dog food?

David: No more Poochy! Now let's get a *little* dog.

Judy: We'd better get a dog big enough to know better.

Now you mustn't think my offspring are all heartless. There were later sad expressions of regret, such as "I liked to play with Poochy," and "Poor, poor Poochy." And "That car shouldn't have runned over our dog." Also, there were awed looks as they viewed the corpse. But without doubt they were most realistic about the whole thing.

Judy is doing nicely at school and is much less shy. On Halloween, two other moms and I were invited to bring cookies and Jello and join the class in a little party. Mrs. Thatcher invited David and Donna too, so they sat with Judy at her table and got to know Billy Foster and the famed Gary Apple. The high spot of the morning was a procession of goblins in paper bag masks they'd pasted themselves. Such ears and ghastly eyebrows!

John is still his same lovable self, more peppy than ever. He painted the house all around in the past few weeks. He's glad to have his parents in California.

Dad is so eager, but he got off on the wrong foot. He banged it on a step he didn't see. He hasn't been able to be on it since they arrived about a week ago. Poor Dad has a lot to learn about farming. It's going to take a lot of whittling to get his ideas down to size. If we can just hold him down until he discovers how much work everything is, maybe he will agree with the rest of us that it will be best just to grow enough for ourselves. It won't be too hard for John and me to get some good licks in for the cause. The trouble has been that Mom is so bossy with him that he often does just the opposite in defiance. We've had lots of built-in cabinets made for their new rooms, which are beginning to look quite nice.

*December 12, 1945*
Dear Girls,

This will be a short letter. Wallpaperers are coming today, and John has invited to supper a couple sailors he ran into. Why? Because one of them knows his uncle John. Mom tells me Jimmie Shively is in town, so I'm going to write him and see if we can get together. Sailors from all over come to San Diego.

Thank you all on behalf of Judy for the birthday cards. And Mom, your box was exciting. The purse is just the thing for her milk or orange juice nickel. The combs, crayons, and candy are always surefire hits. The half dollar, after being thoroughly analyzed as to "how many nickels does it have in it," "how many pennies," etc., was placed in the pig bank for future use. Instead of a birthday party, we had only three children her age for supper. They ate in the living room, the rest of us in the kitchen.

Before she left by plane for Chicago to take a three-month course in designing, Ruby made the kids outfits to match, all in brown linen. The girls' dresses have horizontal lines of white rickrack on the waists. David's bibbed shorts have white buttons on the straps, a white shirt.

# FIFTEEN FAMILY YEARS

When the first year in our new home ended, I was pleased that we had achieved our goals: to establish the "subsistence" farm and to build the two-room-and-porch addition, while keeping the toddlers healthy and happy. I had strengthened ties with Mother and my sisters by starting the Round Robin letters and I had made things ready for John's folks to join us. Mission accomplished! Then came the next fifteen years.

As the war ended, John's job at Standard Iron ended too. At first, he tried selling: Gravelly tractors, then water softeners, but neither attempt was successful. We bought the only tractor. During this time, he dug the trenches for septic tank drainage and painted the house. For money, we sold two lots on our Washington Street frontage. Most of our land faced Anza Street, which was now our address. For something like twenty cents a foot, the county would tar this dirt road. I canvassed our neighbors for their share. All but one paid, but we made up the difference.

Now John contacted the Golden Arrow dairy, thinking it wouldn't be so difficult to sell a product that everyone uses. He had to invest in the milk route and a truck. This worked. He continued with the dairy in a variety of ways for the rest of his working life. While he had the milk route, I did much of the book work, reconciling his notes on costs and receipts each day as well as keeping track of truck payments and expenses. Year-end tax reports were a challenging task. I kept the cow for a few years, for I sold milk to neighbors, along with chickens and eggs.

John had to get up at 5:00 in the morning because the only route available at that time was in Encanto. He didn't get home until 5:30. To have a day off every other week, he had to hire a relief driver. Soon his first truck needed repairs, tires, etc., so he traded it in for a better one. Now we had further debt, so he took no more days off for a while.

When a nearby route became available, he had a shorter day and could even come home for lunch sometimes. Occasionally, through the years, one of the kids rode along with him. According to notes his customers wrote, they appreciated his personal care. For some of them, he'd even put the milk in the fridge if she was going away for the day. He did the same for disabled customers. At Christmas time, he brought home piles of cookies and candy.

One day he had an accident that was featured with a picture in the local newspaper. When he heard the brake give way as he left the truck, he dropped a holder full of milk and raced down the hill to catch the truck. Impossible and dangerous. But even more dangerous, it crashed through a living room just short of a woman in her rocking chair. She wasn't hurt, and she settled with the insurance company after a short-lived threat to sue.

Music has always been a central feature in our family. From the beginning, the children enjoyed singing. They heard my choice of music from a small player, which had been a real bargain. With it came a collection of classics, one symphony from each of eight composers. These 78-rpm records were thick and their playing time was short. It required much running back and forth to turn them over and change them, especially the Cesar Franck long *D Minor Symphony*. In later years, it was a joy to hear those selections played by a live orchestra without interruption.

Soon, I found another great buy, quite unlike anything I see nowadays. It was a series of excellent children's records that didn't talk down to them. There were bits from serious music like one from Haydn's *Surprise Symphony* or his *Toy Symphony*. To this day, the kids all remember their favorite piece, one written especially for children. It was the "Little Brass Band." They played it over and over on their own small player. After Mother spent the winter here, she said that that little brass band kept ringing in her ears for days after she went home and the children always remembered the story:

Early in the morning a trumpet player on a distant hill started the music. He came down into the valley and was joined by a drummer. Then one by one came all the others, a clarinet, an oboe, a flute, two horns, etc. As they came playing into the village children came out and danced in the streets. At the end of the day they played a concert for all the villagers then headed home, still playing as one by one they dropped out.

I have no doubt that this record had an influence on my children. All their lives were connected to music one way or another. David cherished the little toy horn he was given on his fifth birthday. He polished it over and over, washed it, and polished it even more after blowing it. He loved the flute he tried in the elementary school orchestra. We bought him one and he continued it in high school until he switched to oboe. Flutes and oboes were in his life from then on. Like David, Judy continues a profession in music. She started with a little used 48 bass accordion I bought for the kids. She took it to school and played it in the junior high orchestra. After she and a violin player traded instruments overnight, she was forever a violinist. Donna chose the clarinet and a clarinet-playing husband, whom she met in the college orchestra.

All the kids were in marching bands in either junior high or high school. Judy played drums, David and Donna their band instruments. The El Cajon band marched every year in the Mother Goose Parade. They won trophies and went to Pasadena to march in the Rose Parade. They were splendid in their blue-and-gold uniforms with plumed shakos. They became perfectionists to comply with their leader Ben Minor's rigid standards. Not even a touch of white shoe polish could show on the edge of the soles! Of course, the music had to be perfect as well.

Being in concert bands and orchestras was important in many ways. So much time was spent in rehearsals and concerts that high school friends were usually fellow musicians. We parents were close to them and to each other socially. It was a good environment. Judy played in the San Diego Youth Symphony for a while, then she and David played in the Civic Youth Orchestra with an exceptionally fine conductor, Dan Lewis.

By far, the most notable event of 1946 was the birth of Tim on November 15. He was a delight and easy to care for as a lone baby after having two at once as well as a year-old tot. Though he was five years younger than the twins, he had a special place in our family. As he grew older, his grandfather adored him as he tagged along in the garden. When he grew older still, Tim followed siblings to play drums in the marching band. He loved music but played only a harmonica.

Through these years, we often relied on our friend and physician Hugh Frank for medical advice and treatment. The Franks, the Cummings, and the Straubingers began social ties as young struggling families and continued off and on throughout life. When Hugh was our doctor, he discovered David's heart murmur and diagnosed rheumatic fever. David was to remain quite inactive for a while, partly in bed, causing him to miss much of his first school year. He repeated the first grade.

Another need for a doctor happened when Tim was three years old. By that time, Pop and Nana were living in their own home next to ours. Tim had gone freely back and forth. While Nana was visiting me, he had gone over and found some arsenic for snails that she had put "clear at the back of the shelf" in an outdoor cabinet. We knew he had sampled a pill when he came toward home carrying the box. There were fragments on his shirt where he had spit them out. It was awful for him. They had a hard time getting a tube down through his nose. His face turned blue and he made terrifying choking noises. After he vomited, they kept rinsing and rinsing, then gave him an intravenous injection.

Until that incident, we hadn't needed a doctor for a year. Before Hugh left for L.A. for further study, he checked David over with the replacement doctor. They listened to his heart for a long time and agreed that David should do more handwork, replacing most of the strenuous play that boys just can't avoid when they get together. It was an ambiguous situation. Because David didn't feel sick, it was difficult to enforce inactivity on this lively child. I gradually eased the restrictions, and then stopped trying. By and by, the heart murmur and sedimentation rate improved.

Before the spring of 1951, most of the family had good health, except for Donna, who had painful earaches that didn't respond to treatment. She finally had her tonsils removed. There was much misery except for the ice cream. Then in April, we had one dreadful day. Here is how I described it in the Robin:

Most of us had the flu or something of the sort this spring. Judy had a lot of earaches with hers, but it seemed to be in its final stages, so I didn't object to her wanting to sell doughnuts with a group of other Campfire girls in front of Safeway. After all, she just *had* to sell fifty dozen and win a felt badge, especially as she had knocked herself out riding the bike all over the countryside taking orders.

But somehow, she got the time wrong, and about 45 minutes after I had dropped her off in front of the store, she came walking in the door here at home with tears streaming down her face and a look of complete hopelessness. No one had been at the store except for one girl shopping with her mother who said they had sold out a half hour ago.

And poor Judy, despair in her heart and aches in her legs from walking all the way home, still had all those doughnuts to deliver, the ones she had spent many hours taking orders for. As I was soon to discover, they were all scattered up hills and over a three-mile area. She couldn't stop the tears thinking of all that work she still had to do.

I was surprised at a big girl crying like that over a little disappointment and what I thought was a little work, so I took her temperature. It was over 103 degrees! I tucked her in, gave her aspirin, and somehow managed to get all those doughnuts delivered. (Unfortunately, I had outgrown my Campfire uniform some years back!) Perhaps the reason I hadn't noticed sooner in the day that she was sick is that I had been sewing madly to get her skirt done to wear at the booth in front of Safeway. I had barely managed it, too, by not taking time for the snaps but using safety pins instead.

By the time the last doughnut was delivered and I had taken care of Judy, it was time to fix supper. Just as I was about to start— bang! Some neighbors drove in with the limp and lifeless-looking form of David. He had been bike riding by their house up the hill and had missed getting his brakes on and had gone over a six-foot embankment and landed on his head. When Mrs. Foster got to him he was unconscious with his eyes open and his leg curled under him. Imagine her horror!

He regained consciousness though and moaned a little, so they wrapped him in a blanket and brought him home. What a mess he was! He had a big bump on his head and was filthy all over with blood and dirt paste. And all that night we couldn't get a rational word out of him. It was Sunday, so I had a time getting a doctor. I think it was an hour before I got one on the phone. Our regular doctor was in bed with the flu but he told us quiet and warmth is the treatment for shock, so of course he got that. But we did want a doctor to come because of poor Davey's head injury. He was so limp, meany, and miserable.

When a doctor finally came, he gave all the tests for brain hemorrhage, which would be the only real danger. He told us what danger signs to watch for in the pupils of his eyes, a big toe curling under, stupor, etc. He gave Judy a shot of penicillin, prescriptions for nose drops, ear drops, and sulfa pills.

Judy got completely over her trouble without having her tonsils out as Donna had. David slept practically all the next day, and then got OK. But with these brain concussions you have to watch out, so I kept him home all week, Judy until Thursday.

David is responsible for another serious mishap. One day as I was sewing in a room about a hundred feet away from the kids' voices, I heard a sudden alarming scream of dismay. It turned out that it had come from across Anza Street where they had been investigating an abandoned cistern at the back of an elderly woman's property. The kids had found a way to climb up the cement wall, a few feet high, so they could peer down into the cistern a few feet below ground. As David jumped in to see what he could find among the debris there, he landed on some broken glass. I arrived to see blood gushing from his wrist. I don't remember how he got out, but in no time, I had wound something around his wrist. His sisters had raced to get Nana, and we were off to a doctor in her car. Close call and many stitches.

A less serious accident happened when David dislocated his shoulder while pole vaulting. After a few weeks of recuperation, he tried again. Same result. End of high jumping.

Except for these occurrences, the children had good health throughout these years. I had been a stickler for nutrition. I fed them whole grains, many vegetables, and very little sugar.

John had the only serious long-term health problem. Arthritis in his ankles and wrists was followed by sores in his fingers that wouldn't heal. A specialist diagnosed the systemic problem as Raynaud's disease. This circulatory disease keeps blood from flowing freely to fingers and toes. As it advances, it causes hardening of tissues, skin, and/or inner organs. This becomes the rare disease called scleroderma.

Only a month or two ago as I write this, I read something that persuades me that John may have been right when he said afterward that Dr. Frank was wrong to prescribe and administer his remedy, an operation to sever the sympathetic nerve system that causes blood vessels to constrict when subjected to stress, cold, or tobacco. John had to stop smoking immediately. He did. The news article gave no credence to a sympathectomy as a cure for scleroderma.

Without doubt, our good friend Hugh had been eager to make every effort to help John, and he believed the operation would help. However, it was a terrible experience and nearly killed John. My own terror is still a vivid memory. I had gone to his room to wait for him to come up from surgery. It must have been hours from the time I had been given before there was any news. Every time I heard elevator doors open, I would rush out to see peaceful, covered patients one by one being wheeled on by. When John eventually arrived, he was far from peaceful. Hugh was instructing two helpers who were guiding tubes from a suspended apparatus toward John as he thrashed and moaned from the gurney.

It took a while to get him into the bed and fitted with a facial mask hooked up to a tube from the wall, probably pressurized oxygen. By this time, I was leaning against a wall about to faint when Hugh tried to assure me that it would be all right. I learned later that the surgery had taken even longer than expected. And after both doctors had had lunch and the anesthetist had gone home, Hugh went to the recovery room to discover that a leak had caused John to lose so much blood that the other doctor had to be recalled for another operation to repair the leak and administer six pints of blood.

After a period of recovery, when John was being examined he was told to make a fist. He was unable to make the slightest move in his hand. Apparently, in the haste to save his life, his arm had been resting against something that kept blood from reaching the hand. Whatever it was, it took much exercise before he was able to use that hand at all, and the thumb never did become useful. Two or three times a day, I would bend his fingers one at a time toward the palm of his hand. We did this to the tune of "Swan Lake," timing the routine to segments of the music. A therapist came twice a week with an electric device that stimulated nerves to force the fingers to close. Later, my task was reversed; as fingers developed strength, John would try to bend the fingers one by one against my resistance.

Later on, a freak accident did further damage to this hand. He was mowing weeds with our electric mower when I left to get groceries. When I came home and saw the mower standing idly in the field, I assumed he had gone to get gas. Time went by. Then I noticed a bloody rag on the floor and suspected what had happened. Yes, the mower had thrown a wire against him and he had gone for help. Amazingly, Hugh was now working with Dr. Noskins, a hand specialist!

# LIVING AND LEARNING

School was the main occupation during these fifteen years. By 1961, a year of major changes, Judy, Donna, and David had graduated from high school, even though Tim and I had just started high school. He was an El Cajon High School freshman; I was teaching freshmen at El Capitan High School.

It is probably an advantage for a teacher to have had experience with students who have a variety of contrasting abilities and interests. Though all of my children took school seriously, they adapted to it differently. The girls were somewhat more comfortable with books, math, and writing; the boys have always been drawn to opportunities to work with their hands.

Having earned excellent grades, Judy was eighth in her class when she graduated. Bank of America gave achievement awards to graduates in each of the district high schools. Judy won in the Fine Arts section in her school. When winners were invited to round table discussions, she was judged third in the county. She was given a plaque and five hundred dollars. Cal-Western College on Point Loma gave her a scholarship with a job in the library.

Donna did well in school also. Her attitude about school and every other activity was somewhat relaxed but capable and thorough. Whatever she did seemed easy for her. I remember being slightly annoyed at a teacher's repeated comment on her report cards: "Donna gives me no trouble." Not the extent of her qualities!

David had some difficulty learning to read. In those days a new "by sight" method often replaced the phonetic method by which I had learned to read. That may have had something to do with his roadblock. His teacher, Helen Longman, referred us to a colleague who had some useful techniques, which she used with deaf children. This teacher generously gave us some of her time after school to work out the problem. David has always had a full measure of determination to succeed. He was quite successful in woodwork and other shop classes. A teacher said, "Best foreman I ever had."

Tim said later that he wished he had been able to take more shop classes, though he has always enjoyed learning about a wide variety of subjects. His report cards reflect a lackadaisical attitude about doing assignments, but when anything catches his interest, he reads about it avidly. His scores in statewide achievement tests, surprisingly, were many levels higher than anyone expected.

Helen Longman taught several of my kids in the first grade and later had Donna in junior high. Helen became a lifelong friend of our family. I had numerous conversations with her and a couple of other teachers during lunch hours and after school. We talked about politics, school, and national issues.

When Meridian School was built and we transferred there, I again befriended the teachers. Few women had cars at their disposal, but since John used a milk truck, I could use our car. One day, a teacher asked me to take a basket of food that had been collected for a family whose father was in the hospital with TB. I have a vivid memory of this pregnant Mexican mother who told me, "Oh, I wish I wouldn't have any more children!" I regretted that neither the school nurse nor I felt qualified to offer advice.

I was PTA president for two years. One day toward summer, one of the teachers happened to mention that some children dreaded summer vacation. Many were living in small trailers and looked forward only to boredom. That was just too sad! The last day of school had always been delightful for me as I thought ahead to summer fun. When someone mentioned a summer program given by mothers at a Fletcher Hills school, we decided to investigate the possibility of organizing a summer camp at Meridian.

After learning more about the procedures of the other school, we discussed it at a PTA meeting. In no time, we had volunteers eager to help if we went ahead with the plan. First, I called the superintendent, John Montgomery. With his approval, the recreation chairman and I went to a meeting of the school board with copies of a detailed plan. It was agreed that we could do it, but that it would be necessary for the board to hire a certified teacher to be responsible for safety and for care of school property. An athletic coach was hired for us.

It worked beautifully. Several mothers taught ceramics and other handcraft classes. There were games, story hour, hikes, and dramatics. The coach had charge of games and organized a contest in which campers decorated bicycles. After our second year, the superintendent went to the city with the proposition that recreation should be a city responsibility rather than the expense of the school district. There was a state law authorizing a small addition to the tax rate for that purpose. Thus began the Parks and Recreation department of the city of El Cajon. I am pleased to have helped bring this about.

Our ranch was an ideal place for kids to grow up. They turned one of the chicken houses into a workshop. The boys made forts and other projects. We had a variety of pets through the years. There were several cats, Cindy the collie, and Dolce the Chihuahua, a tortoise, and a goat, which scampered with the kids on an outcropping of huge boulders at the edge of our land. And briefly there was even was a seagull that came down from the sky with a broken wing.

From the 1957 Round Robin: "David's horse is going to have a colt any day now. She was pregnant when he bought her, but he had no inkling until someone commented on her condition a couple of weeks ago at a horse show David was attending. Though he managed not to reveal his surprise, you can imagine how shocked and delighted he was.

"He was determined to witness the blessed event. As the time grew near, he slept out by the horse every night in his sleeping bag. Alas, one morning when I came out to the kitchen and looked out, the blessed event had already happened. And there was poor David, sound asleep."

Another excerpt: "David's horse had her colt, the funniest little creature ever. Its legs are toothpicks but how it can run on them! The first day it was left out in the field, it explored madly, for all the world like a two-year-old child. Every time the mother would try to eat a bit of grass, the colt would take off and she'd have to tag along. It would startle at new things and collapse when trying to get away fast." Later: "The colt is growing by leaps and bounds. David takes it along whenever he goes riding, as the mother won't go without it. It's delightful to see the three galloping out of here together, though it worries me to see them out on the road. David gets provoked with me for worrying."

The kids and I spent several years in the 4-H club. I think the agriculture department sponsored and helped the organization. I took a class for leaders in which we learned much about sewing. We learned numerous techniques, like altering patterns to fit. We made tools to aid a tailoring project, either a lined woolen coat or a suit.

We taught girls to sew and to cook. They made dresses and skirts and modeled them in a show at the yearly county fair at Del Mar, vying for blue ribbons and prizes. We also taught cooking and entered the best products for judging. Boys had teachers for carpentry and for raising farm animals. David raised a steer and sold it at the fair.

For a year or two, I was the only El Cajon member of the League of Women Voters. I attended the college area unit of the San Diego League. Then several young women moved into a section of newly built houses and, with an explosion of energy, went about creating an El Cajon unit of the San Diego League of Women Voters.

I remember working in a study committee on trade. I was chair of our "Know Your Town" study and publication. This was required for creating an El Cajon League of Women Voters.

During these years, the children and I attended church and Sunday school at the Unitarian Church of San Diego. I was in charge of a room of preschool children. In the evening, John and I attended a series of lectures called the San Diego Open Forum. We were fortunate to see and hear noted national leaders. A few times, the church organized trips to Ejido el Porvenir in Baja, California. Capable members helped with building and other projects. We brought used clothing and other items.

For several years I worked for the *El Cajon Valley News*. I had met the editor, Si Casady, at the school board meeting, where I got permission for the recreation project. I appreciated the liberal point of view Si expressed in his paper. On an impulse, I clipped a few errors

65

from the paper and put them in an envelope with a note: "Let me help you make a good paper perfect; I'm a good proofreader."

He answered, "You don't want to work here; I can't pay much." But I did want to, and as time went on, I also edited copy and wrote headlines. Once I did a whole page for the home section. I took our photographer to take pictures of a tiny lake for fishing and swimming that had been created by friends of mine by dredging a low spot on their land and adding sand.

This part-time job was perfect for me. The paper was published only three times a week, and I worked only half days. I enjoyed the company and the work; the kids were in school. In addition to money from this job, I made a little more from piano lessons—$1.50 each. As John's health became worrisome, it was clear that I could never make both ends meet with work like this.

Now I had an urgent reason for finishing college: to get a teacher's credential. I enrolled in two courses at San Diego State College. I decided to see whether I could still handle college-level studies. Realizing that my best chance of success would be to start with subjects most interesting to me at that time: "Europe in the Twentieth Century" and "Social Psychology." No problems. Next semester I took three courses, then kept going until I developed a problem with my back that almost destroyed the venture. Perhaps I had hunched over the books too intensely, for the pain in my upper back radiating down my arms became extremely painful. I was taking three aspirins at a time every few hours and through the night. The doctor in the health clinic at college tried muscle relaxing pills, diathermy, and other remedies, all with no relief.

When it was time to register for the second semester of my last year, I hesitated to enroll and pay the fee: I was afraid I couldn't go on. John said I shouldn't worry about wasting money. Go ahead and enroll. If I then dropped out, so what! I had been in touch all along with our friend Dr. Frank to let him know whether anything was working. Finally, he insisted that I make an appointment with a neurologist he knew. After a brief look at the X-rays I had brought from the clinic, he knew exactly what to do. He prescribed a traction device. That did it. The first night of use, I was able to skip the aspirin and go ahead. I added three years to my Bluffton two and earned BA and MA degrees and a teaching credential by 1961 when I started teaching.

During these years, Nana and Pop became settled in their own home next to ours. Their plan was to start with a double-wide garage and live in it while Pop built a house. We sold them a piece of land adjacent to our house. That reduced our debt to them. Despite his being deaf and without building experience, Pop did amazingly well in learning what he needed to know and how to get needed help. Sometimes he did plumbing and electrical work himself, requiring only inspection, advice, and legal approval from men with licenses. He laid most of the cement blocks himself. Soon the "garage" design was modified so much with windows and other refinements that this became their permanent home. A single car garage was added.

Their presence had many mutual benefits. The grandparents had far more pleasure with their grandchildren than I have had with mine, for they saw each other day after day. This closeness was a gift for the kids, too. I love the picture of little Tim tagging along with Pop as he gardened. We still have samples of ceramics the kids made during their many sessions with Nana, who took classes to learn all the techniques, from raw clay through firing. She was always available for childcare or for her car when needed.

We had frequent suppers together where Nana told about her activities. She took a class in hat making; she was active in a Republican club. I doubt if we debated politics. Pop was usually silent at supper; not often enough, there was a lull in the conversation, which allowed for penciled responses and questions. One difficult stretch of time occurred before they had moved from our house. Nana had stood on a chair to reach a top drawer and broke her leg. For weeks, she got around on a straight chair fitted with a wooden extension to support her leg.

Dad never lost interest in gardening. He couldn't bear to waste anything, sometimes to Mom's annoyance. She had to make use of every scrawny vegetable. Because the ranch had numerous wine grapes, Dad looked up directions for making wine. He bought the necessary equipment and fulfilled the requirement for recording his intention. Imagine the inspector's amusement when he came and saw what a tiny production was taking place! The final product was delicious wine vinegar!

Four times, my mother and stepfather came for the winter. They rented a motel or apartment and once a trailer to pull into our backyard. Their presence enriched our lives in many ways. We enjoyed small trips with them. Mother helped me with cooking, sewing, and house chores. Twice, she helped select and hang wallpaper. Her pizzas outshone any I've ever tasted. She and Webster liked showing slides of places they visited on their way here. Webster drove slowly and took excellent care of his cars, which he liked to renew every two or three years. Twice we bought his old but perfect Chrysler and Ford Galaxy.

Not until Tim was five did it become practical to introduce my family to the joys of camping. For one thing, we finally owned a car that could drive us up to the mountains. John was not particularly eager to go camping. His previous experience had been with large, organized YMCA groups, so he had trouble envisioning a family expedition. Besides, we had neither camping equipment nor the money to buy any. However, to make the most of a small expenditure was a challenge for me. I said, "Suppose I invest a total of $50.00 for a short tryout camping trip to Black Canyon, and then if it doesn't work out we'll just drop the idea for awhile. OK?" "OK," said John.

Here is what I bought with my $50.00 (Remember, this was in 1951 and inflation hadn't risen too far): My first and most expensive purchase was an icebox. I bought a kapok double-wide pad on which three kids could spread out crosswise. With a few large safety pins, I used blankets to concoct sleeping bags. To make them warm, I inserted newspapers between the folds, an idea I'd read about. Then I got a little Indian tepee in which the girls could change clothes. And finally, in a half gallon thermos I had bought for twenty-five cents at the Junior League rummage sale, I brought along a beef stew with vegetables.

It was late in the day and getting dark and gloomy when we descended into Black Canyon. Some of the children were feeling apprehensive as the road curved down and down. Then when we reached the campground, we were greeted with a sign saying, "DRY CAMP. NO WATER." What a start! How could I now sell camping to my family? We decided to have supper and sleep in this deserted place and then go up to Cuyamaca State Park tomorrow.

With the beef stew, milk from the icebox, and melted ice cubes, we had supper and eventually tried to sleep. Newspapers I had folded into the sleeping bags were not a good idea. They made a crackling noise when anyone changed position, raising alarms about rattlesnakes. Then came flashes of light across the sky. "That's called heat lightning," said John. "It never rains here in August." Alas, it did, a little. The tepee wasn't waterproof, but it helped. So did the car.

Next morning, we decided to look around before heading for the state park. Rain had cleaned and sparkled the trees. The sun came out; white fluffy clouds adorned the blue sky. And, to our delight, we were not the only campers after all. A young couple was honeymooning nearby. They seemed glad to see us, especially Kelly, the bride. Gordon could hardly wait until we had breakfast so he could show us around.

There was water after all. The stream that had gone underground was flowing nicely upstream a bit. And Kelly insisted on sharing drinking water with us until we produced some. As John and Gordon brought water from the stream, the kids gathered sticks to make a fire. I filtered the water through a clean dish towel before putting it on to boil.

It required many brave and cautious steps beside enormous boulders to follow a path up to a large, deep pool. The guys swam in it while the kids waded in the shallow end. We had lunch under a tree along the shore. So it turned out that we had a great adventure after all. Our problems didn't dismay John at all; he enjoyed the pioneering, the make-do aspects of it.

From then on, camping became our favorite family activity, especially hiking and exploring. We took advantage of all the nearby campgrounds. The kids liked searching for the best sites wherein to pitch our tent. We developed routines for setting up camp, cleaning the ground of cigarette butts, and leaving each site better than we found it. I found sturdy cotton in four different colorful patterned materials for campers to cover thin foam pillows and to make tote bags with drawstrings for their things.

When we went to Borrego, we studied library books about desert plants and geology in the tent by lantern light. The next day, we looked for rock samples and followed a path that helped us identify a delightful variety of small trees, bushes, and flowering plants. This path led upward beside a stream toward an oasis of palm trees.

When we got together later, we enjoyed reminiscing about special times we'd enjoyed together, in Zion, the Grand Canyon, and Sequoia.

Mishaps were fun to remember, like the time several inches of Utah mud soaked our sleeping bags and other gear. Before returning a rental car to pick up ours, which had been taken to a mechanic for minor repairs, it had looked as if it might rain. So I put down the flap of our umbrella tent. We returned from the garage to find that, instead of protecting the tent, the flap had served as a funnel for the rain! Red Utah dirt came through the open door to join inches of water on the floor, soaking all our ready-to-go gear. Rescuing enough bath towels to soak up the mud, we formed a line to pass muddy towels along to those who would wring them out and send them back to soak up more mud.

A letter to Mother describes an even more memorable trip:

On the Easter weekend, we went to a campsite in the desert, and oh what an experience! The wind was like a hurricane. The tent went down before nightfall, so we managed to tie it to the shelter for a windbreak to protect four of us (we thought) while two slept in the car. But David and I were constantly beaten by the thing. John and Donna were under the table. We had to keep our heads down inside the sleeping bags or get a face full of sharp, tiny stones or sand. Sleep was out of the question. Our only worry was: will gravity be enough to keep us from blowing away? Everything else did blow away, even shoes. Once, during a sort of lull, someone managed to run to the car to find from Judy's watch whether it was morning. It was only 10:30!

Several hours later, I was so cold I decided to make a break for the car. As I couldn't untie the strings of my sleeping bag, which I had tied to the shelter, I had to go without it. When I got to the car, I found nary a scrap of a coat or anything warm, so I pulled Tim in his sleeping bag on top of me. In spite of the constant swaying and vibrating of the car, I finally fell asleep to a dream I had pneumonia. I awoke and shifted Tim off my chest and dreamed I had broken legs.

When morning came at last, what a sight greeted us! Our tent was down. It was still blowing madly. We recovered some of our pans, clothes, etc., from the cactus bushes. It was an hour before I found two matching shoes. Our icebox was blown over and full of sand. Goodness knows how it got in. All the food in the cupboard except canned goods was too sandy to use. Somehow we managed to eat what passed for breakfast.

When we had the car worked on later, they overhauled the generator, starter, etc., all permeated with sand. The windshield was permanently etched. We were able to start home just as it began to rain. Coming through the Lagunas, we ran into a snowstorm. Many cars had stalled or were afraid to move in the inch of snow. Probably they had never tried to drive in the snow before. We were about an hour going one mile. Our starter wasn't working right, and the repeated stopping made the motor stall. We had to just sit there and wait for the starter to work, which it would after about five minutes. What a relief when we got past the snow.

As they were growing up, the children had the usual concerns of their age. They earned their spending money in various ways, including babysitting by the girls and helping the painting contractor across the street by the boys. Once David amazed Si Casady, the newspaper editor, by completely taking apart a linotype machine he had bought at a fire sale, cleaning all pieces, and perfectly reassembling it. He and Mark Casady also raised a plot of sweet corn for sale.

They bought some of their own clothes, but I helped as much as I could. I recall buying a ten-yard bolt of pinwale dark green corduroy and ten yards of red and green plaid gingham with which I made a plain skirt, a full skirt, a lined jacket, a blouse, and a dress. This created many coordinated outfits. But when I bought all the material to make something else, I realized that ready-made clothes were just as cheap. One absurd fad, thankfully brief, had the girls ironing extremely full petticoats every morning. Most important was something to wear to school dances or proms. It was a pleasure to see them dressed becomingly.

One period, shortly before I started college, I felt so upset by John's various difficulties and by turmoil I was experiencing with Judy that I went for weekly visits to a counselor in Family Service Association. Though details of my concerns are dim, I do remember that he gradually eased my distress. After sending me to a psychologist for tests, he encouraged me to go ahead with college plans. Recently I asked Judy what she remembers of those days. She said, "Oh, I was just a *teenager!*"

Our family's saddest loss in this period was the death of John's father, George Washington Straubinger, in 1960, the day before his birthday, February 2, and that of another special man, the one for whom he was named and was celebrated with Dad's annual cherry pie. We all missed Pop's love of life and his never-ending kindness. Though he had gradually weakened, his final illness was mercifully brief.

As these fifteen years came to an end, our farm had dwindled, most school days had ended, most health problems had been taken care of, and family fun had become memories. My life was almost half over, and the next half would contrast greatly. It is remarkable how so many changes took place in the fall of 1961 with dramatic suddenness.

Donna dropped out of college and married Wayne Gruenewald. Barbara Frank gave her a shower. She was lovely in her long white gown in a ceremony at the Unitarian Church with a reception afterward in Bard Hall. Judy had dropped out of college and was working at a television station. And I had managed to get a teaching position at El Capitan High School!

As for David, an impulse of mine had a life-changing result. As a member of the Women's Concert Association, I got an invitation to the home of Hugh Matheny's mother to hear him play a piano and his oboe. My time was completely absorbed in preparing for my first year of teaching, and I knew that oboe players have some unique common interests, so I took the liberty of calling Mrs. Matheny and asking if my oboe-playing son might come instead.

She may have regretted her assent, for the two oboists usurped much of the afternoon talking oboe together. Hugh, a teacher in the Jordan School of Music in Indianapolis, was spending summer vacation here. He and David spent much of that time together. At the beach on the last day, Hugh delivered an amazing offer. Though he realized that David was planning to continue studies at junior college the next month, he could have a scholarship at Jordan if he should ever change his plans. Would he! In short time, a confirming phone call plus a plane ticket took David away from home forever.

All this within a week or two! A suddenly shrunken family and a new role in a different scene made the next act in my life story a real contrast to the first.

# TEACHING YEARS (1961-1978)

As I prepared to face four roomfuls of freshmen a day, I felt shaky and unready. Though I had no anxiety in front of adult groups and I had dealt easily with groups of youngsters, this was different. These kids also had qualms when they entered high school. They needed me to be a confident and reassuring partner.

Practice teaching had helped a little. I had started by gradually taking over a junior-high English class. Then, under a supervising teacher, I taught geography to a freshman class. And while I was still taking education classes, the Ford Foundation had a program to evaluate the use of aides in the classroom. It employed another woman and me for a year to help a team of two history teachers with routine chores and their time-taking creative ideas. This was a valuable way to see if principles taught in education classes worked in real life. Over lunch, we two helpers made evaluations of our own.

But I was now alone to deal with what I needed to teach and who I needed to teach it to—four classes a day, later five. To say this was exhausting would be quite an understatement. Back home after a day was over, I would fall on my bed and practically die. I suppose this is when my blood pressure became a lifelong problem. At lunchtime, I overheard some teachers discussing transcendental meditation (TM) as a way to relax. I joined a class; it helped.

Even though my major had been social science, the only openings for teachers were in English. Before the women's lib movement in the later sixties, it seemed natural at El Capitan for the social studies department to consist entirely of men while women were all in the English department. Teaching history required a good voice for lecturing, and the subject provided a stock of multiple choice and true/false items for easy test grading. This made history or government a good choice for guys. English teaching, on the other hand, required hours of detailed work to read student essays and to improve writing, along with requiring perhaps a more sensitive appreciation of literature. These requirements made English seem a better fit for women.

Happily, after my first two years, I was privileged to become part of an excellent exception to this analysis. The American Studies program was a departure from the usual way of scheduling courses and planning curriculum. Paul DeKock started the program after leaving for a year to attend Harvard and become inspired with this way to blend history and English courses. Our innovative superintendent made it possible to establish this program at El Capitan.

Paul, Dave Yount, and I worked with about 120 juniors in a two-period block of time. A different practice teacher each year worked with us. We had access to a room large enough for all 120 students in addition to the usual classrooms. Paul led us in organizing three-week blocks of time per unit of study. Sometimes we brought everyone together for a lecture aided by two large screens, an overhead projector, and slides. Typically, one screen contained an outline, with pictures on the other. We had a variety of other programs with student participation.

In some periods, half of our students did exercises or took tests in the big room while the other half were divided into four groups small enough to meet around tables for discussion. We coordinated works of literature with historical periods. We blended writing and discussion skills with each topic.

Team teaching made for flexibility and innovative ideas. I found the years working with Paul and Dave to be my most satisfying teaching years. I enjoyed our planning and rehashing sessions as we learned from each other. Each of us had different strengths.

I developed ways of transforming grammar instruction into lessons for sentence improvement. Instead of drills to learn parts of speech, structures, diagramming, and other grammar concepts, we worked directly with the students' own work. We saved their writings through the year in folders. We graded them on what they said, not how they said it, then later in the year we pulled out their compositions to use as raw material for lessons on better ways to put sentences together. A teacher would pencil "S" alongside sentences that could be improved by using the better structures we now taught. We teachers noted whatever else should be given later attention. We could prescribe specific exercises in the textbook as needed, individually or for the class.

Perhaps our most exciting new activities were the simulations. These involved role-playing in a way that brought to life situations faced by people in various historical periods. The first one we used was "Disunia." Each student assumed a role as governor, official, or congressperson from a different state as they struggled to resolve differences and write the 1789 constitution. Other simulations related to the civil war ("Division"), to labor-management relations ("Strike"), and to racial problems ("Sunshine"). Students earned points, or grades, by choices they made as members of these periods. This was motivating for our more able students, but some others found it confusing.

As enrollment grew and a new high school was necessary, El Capitan High School split our student body with Santana High School. Paul and Dave taught American Studies there while I teamed with Sandy Long in a group for which simulations were not practical. The American Studies course was designed for college-bound students. Sandy and I used a stripped-down version for our AA (applied arts) classes. In addition to American Studies, I also taught various English classes.

For a while, the English department practiced a unique program to encourage students to read more self-chosen literature. Each teacher chose a novel or two to put on a reading list of available books. We gave this list to students of English classes throughout the school. They were to choose a book, read it, and meet with whichever teacher would be leading a discussion of that book on Reading Seminar Day. This scrambling of English classes took place every other Monday. Students either participated in a seminar devoted to a particular book or went to an English study hall to read or write. This mixing of students and teachers and all classes, freshmen to seniors, gave everyone a unique experience.

In meetings of the English department, we often considered other ways of meeting a wide variety of interests and abilities. So, in addition to required courses, we wanted to offer elective courses. We would work on basic reading and writing skills throughout. Course offerings might include speech, advanced composition, poetry, science fiction, mythology, shop English, journalism, or fiction writing. As our weekly department meetings didn't allow enough time to build this plan, we decided to apply for a grant from the district's innovation fund so that we could hire substitute teachers for a few days, allowing us time to meet and develop the plan.

I was given the job of writing the application and reporting on our activities. We were granted $500 but used only $225. As I later reported, "We often traded or combined classes among ourselves rather than bring in substitutes who would be less likely to understand what we wanted done in our classes, but knowing we had the option of using the substitutes, if we chose to, seemed to energize us."

Once I came upon a Robert Frost poem in an anthology we were using. Since poetry was not a strong point with me, I made it a practice to use only those poems that I myself really connected with. This poem was "Out, Out," the title of which came from a line in Shakespeare's Macbeth which reads, "Out, out, brief candle!" Frost's poem tells of a boy who has an accident with a buzz saw, losing his hand, and then his life. One moment all is well, an ordinary day. An instant later, "he saw all spoiled." The poem ends with these lines:

No one believed. They listened at his heart.
Little—less—nothing!—and that ended it.
No more to build on there. And they, since they
Were not the one dead, turned to their affairs.

As I read this poem to my several classes of high school juniors, I was living back in the seventh grade on March 28, 1930.

In 1965, I applied for an NDEA fellowship. The National Defense Education Act was a reaction to Russia's launching of Sputnik, the first space satellite. Alarmed that the U.S. was falling behind in scientific achievement, the government quickly created educational programs to boost our scientific ability. Later it was persuaded that study in humanities was important as well as science, so English programs were added. That was just what I needed. As I was teaching mostly English classes, I wanted to earn an English major to add to my social science major. I was accepted by the institute at St. Cloud, Minnesota. The very generous NDEA program paid tuition, travel, and living expenses as well as a family stipend when needed.

I thoroughly enjoyed this summer between differing teaching years. It started with the plane ride. I'd had only one earlier flight, a short one to San Francisco for a League of Women Voters convention. I described the ride to my family:

Dear John and all,

Has it been only two days since that gratifying send-off at the airport? It feels so much longer, especially since the candy is more than half gone already!... As you know, I sat at the tail end of the plane, supposedly the safest spot. The view was unobstructed and dazzling. Almost before your good-byes stopped ringing in my ears, I was looking down at Inspiration Point in the Lagunas, mountains on one side and desert on the other. The speed with which we overleapt highway 80 was dazzling. I had to look fast not to miss anything, in spite of the wide radius of vision.

I especially enjoyed the color schemes: a rich, live olive green along with much blackish earth color ringed with magenta and accented by blocks of mustard fields. These colors lie in geometric patterns like Mondrian paintings.

I kept wishing I had a talkative geologist for a seat partner; for I kept seeing strange formations, like an isolated blob of dark volcanic mountains and a sudden switch from peaked shape to flattened liver lobes. The rivers made patterns like those World Book pictures of the human circulatory system.

All along the way, I was so excited that I kept reaching for more of Tim's M&M's. It was a childish reflex like nail-biting. Alas, as soon as the air became rocky over Denver, I had to reach for the little bag. A friendly neighbor advised, "Look at a fixed spot on the horizon and breathe deeply," but he was too late.

I arrived safely at the college, but for two days, my baggage languished in the Fargo Greyhound station while I chewed my nails in anguish, made hysterical phone calls, and even at night, I had to get dressed in my suit to take a trip to the bathroom! At first, the manager of the St.

Cloud station said there was nothing to do until "tracers" had borne fruit. But when I asked for the name of the Minneapolis manager to see what could be done at that point, he switched his line from "nothing to do but wait" to "I'll save you the price of a call and phone him myself." And lo, the next time I was able to call, the bags were there.

Now to the good part, which far over-shadowed airsickness and bag loss. It was an ideal six weeks. The professors were excellent; the literature and composition course were meaty and well planned; fellow students were congenial and intelligent. I could see the Mississippi from my dorm window; in ten minutes I could walk across a bridge to a park on the other side. We had two delightful side trips. One week, we rode north to Moorehead, another Minnesota college, where we had a course in understanding abstract poetry, something which usually eludes me. Another trip was to the Guthrie Theater in Minneapolis where we saw Chekhov's "The Cherry Orchard."

In 1971, after teaching various English and history classes, I was granted a sabbatical year for pursuing a Masters degree. This year was packed with challenging academic classes and requirements as well as time to work on a rather ambitious dream of developing our two acres of land. When I returned to El Capitan the following year, the history classes had been taken over by new teachers. California had started a new policy of requiring new teachers to teach only in their majors, but I still had a general secondary credential with no such restriction. Therefore, I was assigned geography and black history classes. I refurbished my limited geography knowledge in the summer at Grossmont College.

After two years, I joined the faculty of the new Valhalla school. Because of a delay in building this unique high school, we were allowed to share rooms with Granite Hills for one semester. For two years at Valhalla, I was in another American Studies team. Teachers who had helped design the new floor plan had made it easy to have more flexible activities. With four classroom spaces close together in a "pod," we could quickly rearrange groups. The school's large open space with library was good for independent study and assignments. There were small rooms with screens for movies or other audiovisual presentations. Instead of seats, students would sit on carpeted stairs.

Then, at last, it became possible for me to have classes in government, but by now I was in my late fifties and five thirty-five-student classes a day had become too tiring. My first remedy was to whittle it down to three classes a day. The blessed principal agreed, and a lowered salary was now not a problem. For two years, I was able to try my ideas for personalizing education. I had concentrated on that during my sabbatical year.

By staying in school all day but having three free periods, I was able to schedule appointments with students who weren't "getting it." At the start of each unit of study, I gave the class a list of things to know and be able to do. I matched a test to these objectives. Sadly, I had found it necessary to make tests cheat-proof. After grading them, I did an item analysis to reveal what I needed to review. Then I gave a second similar test over the same material.

Having assumed that students had learned more about government in earlier grades, I was surprised to discover how much they didn't know. This appalled me, for I agreed with a quotation saying that civilization is a race between education and disaster (A League of Women Voters perspective!). I discovered the nature of these knowledge gaps when I made appointments with the students who didn't do well on the makeup tests.

Typically, five or six would meet with me around a table and with their test papers in front of me; I discussed missed items with them. Although they wouldn't ask "silly" questions in the large class, here, among others with similar problems, they were glad to clear up any misconceptions or whatever they hadn't understood.

These little seminars were a joy for me, and some kids liked them too. One girl said she learned more in one or two of these discussions than she could get in a whole semester of regular classes. I always found it difficult to make lesson plans fitting both those who already knew most of the material and those who lacked the background or who found it puzzling.

With this system, I was able to pass all seniors with a "C" or better. They could earn higher grades by what they wrote about current news items, or columns relating to government activities that I brought to class. Each clipping related to the current topic was attached to a sheet of paper on which the student wrote his or her name after reading it. I went through the pile of clippings to see which had the most readers and added some optional questions about that clipping at the end of the test.

After two years of this, I was even more certain that one-on-one-type education was the way to go. Lectures, films, and books are indispensable, but for digestion, they need to be followed up with personal dialogue. Now I had an idea for a new way to retire. I would teach what amounted to only ONE class a day. At Valhalla, we had "A-B" days. Some classes would meet Tuesdays and Thursdays, others on Wednesdays and Fridays. Periods were twice as long, with short ones on Mondays. I would teach a total of thirty-five students, or one class load, with a 20% salary. I would stay all day twice a week. Some periods, I might take a few students from an overloaded class. In other periods, there might be a small group who needed make-up or remedial work. Or, as I had done previously, I'd work with one or more students on a subject for which there was no class offered. I had done this once before when a boy wanted to study international relations. He dreamed of being a photojournalist. We compiled a reading list, enrolled him in "special study," and arranged a time for us to discuss what he'd learned.

I wrote my plan on a single sheet of paper and took it to the principal. He was genuinely interested. This scheme could solve some scheduling problems. It would be a bargain financially and might even lead to ideas for other gradual retirement opportunities. "Could I keep this paper?" he asked. "Of course, that's what it's for," said I.

Alas, it was not to be. By the next year, he had become superintendent of the entire Grossmont High School district and his replacement principal at Valhalla had scuttled A-B days for the conventional system, making my plan impossible.

# OTHER DOINGS

During the first years of this period, John changed jobs several times. Because of his health problems, he sold the milk route. Golden Arrow Dairy opened a drive-in store on Mission Gorge Road. John was manager there for a while and then at the company's short-order restaurant in Chula Vista. In both of these jobs, he still had to handle cold bottles and ice cream.

As I wrote in the Round Robin, "There just wasn't anything available he could do without handling cold things, so he has ended up in a semi-clerical *half-time* job! At least he gets half-time pay, although you know John; he manages to spend full time doing it. He has always believed in giving his boss twice as much as he's being paid for. I persuaded him to pick up some specialized skill or other, but when he went to see about it, the deadline for this semester had passed. In the meantime and for some time to come, I'm afraid our newly won solvent condition has once more disappeared."

In a year or two, this half-time job became a good full-time position as route supervisor/public relations employee. Because he had had a route himself, and because he had always had good rapport with his customers, with an effective way of handling problems, he functioned well in this spot until he retired.

Though problems with his cold hands disappeared, he had two other setbacks during these years. One was a bad back sprain in '65, requiring the use of a hospital bed and the same traction device I had used. It was attached to a heavy corset and hooked over the foot of the bed. In my case, it had been a chin strap hooked over the head of the bed. He was out of work for a month. Dr. Smith came to the house.

Doctors and tests led to a diagnosis that his worrisome weight loss and anemia were caused by scar tissue in his esophagus, making it difficult for food to go through. This scar was the result of an accident years ago, when he had sleepily gone to the kitchen for a drink of water and made the mistake of reaching for a glass into which David had added Clorox to soak his oboe reeds. Four painful sessions with a dilation procedure helped make a smoother passageway for food.

With few exceptions, the next seventeen years were free of health problems. They were some of the best times of our lives.

During these years, Judy lived at home off and on. For the rest of her life, she concentrated on her skill as a violinist, whatever else she was doing. She worked at television stations both in San Diego and, for several years, in San Francisco. For a while, she did my old proofreading job at the *El Cajon Valley News*. In September '65, when she finally decided on a major, she enrolled in the biology sequence at the new UCSD campus in La Jolla.

About that time, she went to a party for musicians where she met Myrl Hendershott, an oceanography professor at UCSD. Three months later in a letter to Mother, I described the simple ceremony at the Unitarian church where the Hendershotts were married! As I told Mother, "We liked Myrl very much. He's rather quiet, good natured, serious, young looking (he's 26, same as Judy). He plays organ at a Congregational church and is also an excellent pianist. His Italian mother used to be an opera singer." Juliet, the Hendershotts' only daughter and my fourth grandchild, was born in 1969.

As Donna and Wayne had been married shortly before the beginning of the fire season, Wayne continued his summer job as firefighter. They lived in a trailer at Lake Henshaw when Karl was born. For years afterward, he taught band music and English at Julian High School, then in Bishop when Gail was born. Karl was my first grandchild, Gail my second.

When Wayne decided high school teaching was not for him, he resigned and took computer courses at Coleman College in San Diego. As soon as he finished, he was employed as a teacher there. Soon he became a computer programmer in a variety of defense and government jobs. The family lived in La Mesa, Santee, El Cajon, Salt Lake City, and Maryland, where he worked for the state department. While they were in El Cajon, Donna worked in the credit department at Sears and then in the media center for El Cajon elementary district. When they finally came back to El Cajon, Donna resumed work in the media center until she and Wayne retired.

David had no sooner settled in Indiana than he applied for and was awarded a scholarship at the Juilliard School of Music in New York City. He studied with Harold Gomberg, probably the top oboist in the country. When the Indianapolis Symphony Orchestra needed an oboe player, they asked Gomberg for a recommendation. He chose David, who happily returned to the place where he had made close friends, including a fellow musician, Helen Williams. They were soon married.

After several years of traveling with the orchestra, David left it to stay with his family, which by then included Melissa, my third grandchild, born in February '67 during the Vietnam War. Perhaps this birth helped protect him from being drafted. In July of the previous year, I had written, "We are holding our breath about David; lately there have been articles in the paper about the possibility of revising draft procedures so that they will take older men. (How strange to think of David as being 'older'!)"

Unfortunately, our younger son Tim was not spared. He had basic training in San Diego as a Navy man in '66. I wrote in the Robin, "I hate this war, and I'm sure it isn't just because of Tim. It is so senseless. We can't do what we're trying to do, but I don't know how we're going to wiggle out of the trap we fell into." I also enclosed excerpts from Tim's letters: "Your letters made me very homesick, but it's the only thing that makes me feel alive or different here ... Gregg's letter made me so homesick I almost cried and I couldn't finish it till night when I knew I could if I wanted to." And then, "Two men in our company fainted and one was discharged ... Another boy's father died recently and he kept stuttering and wetting his bed. So he was sent to a psychiatric ward and discharged ... But don't worry about me. I'm OK." From San Diego, he went to Connecticut to submarine school. He was on a nuclear submarine for four years.

It had been so nice having him home making beautiful things with his pottery wheel, but as I told my sisters in the Robin,

> It's really calm and peaceful not to have any kids around and I can't say I would wish to have any of them back except him. And since he's the messiest around the house, I wouldn't mind his being gone either if it were somewhere that would be good for him. But to be in a war machine is more than I can bear without getting sick whenever I think about it.
>
> I have to say I hate Johnson for getting us so deeply into this adventure. When we went to Tim's graduation, there was a piece in the program about this top guy out there being the one who invented napalm. I felt icy thinking about human beings bragging about a horrible invention like that … How can we bear it when we realize that we ourselves in America—all of us—are responsible for napalming people in their own country!

As I read the following paragraphs from a later Robin, I feel that these comments on war are every bit as true today:

> I have just read an extremely interesting essay by Simone Weil, an intelligent French woman who died at age thirty-four. She uses the *Iliad* to show what the use of force does to dehumanize people, making them almost helpless "things"—regardless of whether they are defeated or victorious.
>
> In a war, people get caught up in the momentum of the thing and become emotionally incapable to think what would be the best course of action—what kind of settlement to make with the enemy—because by this time they have committed so much effort and so many lives to the war that they won't settle for less than victory lest all the previous fighting can be considered a waste (which it probably was).

My blood pressure continued to be quite high through my teaching years. Also, I had a hysterectomy, bursitis in both shoulders, and a puzzling problem with my inner ear. The first time I had this extreme vertigo, Dr. Hugh Frank put me in the hospital for tests. The slightest movement of my head made the room seem to whirl uncontrollably. I suppose it was Dramamine that finally eased that. A few years later, I had another extreme episode and was sent to an ear specialist. He took about a dozen tests, probably suspecting a brain tumor.

Again, I was sent to a hospital, this time to test that theory. I remember coming out of the anesthetic to overhear Hugh with a neurologist, the ear doctor, and the man who had done the test as they studied the X-ray picture. The neurologist said the lesion was in a part of the brain where it wouldn't grow fast, so he counseled "wait and see." So we waited and saw. From time to time, I had slight dizzy spells, but Dramamine helped. In a few years, we forgot all about it. This neurologist, bless his heart, was the same one who had solved the back problem that had almost caused me to drop out of my final semester before graduation. The traction apparatus he prescribed had rescued me from shoulder and upper back pain, which dozens of aspirins couldn't relieve.

Summers were enjoyable during these years. Judy lived nearby and sometimes she gathered large groups of relatives for picnics under the widely spreading trees in the Hendershott back yard. Cousin Christopher did magic shows. Children gathered Easter eggs, beautiful works of art that had been produced during a previously delightful occasion. Several times, David's family came by plane. They joined John at our house during the entire time I was studying in the St. Cloud NDEA course.

Once I persuaded John to go the opposite direction. The family had celebrated—and undergone—a few changes by then. Shortly after the birth of Melissa, when Helen had just begun to drive her car, she suffered a frightful accident. A car rounded a corner too fast and smashed into hers; she broke her leg and hip. Thank God for seat belts!

For a while, she was in an extensive cast, so they had to get people to help care for the baby. David's business hadn't progressed far enough to meet expenses without great difficulty, but they managed. When the insurance company finally settled two years later, they had recovered enough for a down payment on their house. Then came another celebration: Joel was born in 1970.

This letter shows how I persuaded John to go for a visit.

Dear Helen and David,

What clever plotters you are! That picture of Joel was just the thing to provide the final convincing argument to John that he should come and see you. I had been working on him ever since you first suggested the idea, but he was always ready with an excuse like, "I can't get away from the dairy that soon," or "I don't want to take a vacation without you," or even, "I'm afraid to fly alone." (Facetiously, of course.) He finally got around to asking the office manager about some time off in May. Then Joel's picture provided the clincher, shifting him from "maybe" to "OK".

Twice John and I drove to visit Donna and Wayne when they were living in Bountiful, a suburb of Salt Lake City. We split the drive in two by reserving a motel room in Las Vegas. That proved helpful on our way home after one trip. I had broken my ankle on a hike during our last day there. Donna took John and me to a trail on a wooded hill. All went well; I even have a photo that shows me walking on a log while I adventurously crossed a rushing stream. No accident there, but back on the easy trail, I twisted my ankle on wobbly pebbles and broke it in two places. Donna and John supported me as I hopped the short way down to the car.

An X-ray confirmed the break. The clinic doctor taped the foot, fitted me with crutches, and gave me pain pills. She said the bones couldn't be set until the swelling went down, so I should wait for that until I got home. We made an appointment with Kaiser (our HMO) and left early the next morning. John drove as I sat in the back with my leg stretched out on the seat. The crutches worked well when we stopped for lunch. In the middle of the night in the Las Vegas motel, I awoke, listened to John's light breath, and whispered, "Are you awake?" "Yes," he said, "let's go." We did, and by following a truck's rear light, we were able to follow winding roads and get to Kaiser as they opened.

From the time I met Si and worked for the *El Cajon Valley News*, the Casady family and ours became good friends. The paper had passes to symphony concerts, giving Si's wife Virginia and me many wonderful evenings under the stars in Balboa Park. I gave piano lessons to their sons Cort and Lance. I was pleased when music became part of Cort's career. All the family came to our house for traditional Christmas carol parties. It was always Si's booming "Five Golden Rings" when we sang "The Twelve Days of Christmas." We learned a new carol every year.

One day, the phone rang with Virginia's voice from Guatemala. She said there was to be a special music week there in Antiqua and I had to come and help her enjoy it. I did, joyfully. The Casadys lived for a year in an amazing home with a beautiful garden adjacent to the high wall of an old cathedral, making a charming view from the balcony outside my upstairs room.

A few well known musicians from the New York Philharmonic who came for two days of the musical events also stayed in the Casady house. Annie, a young woman from Oklahoma, spent much time with us. She was living as a native person in a tiny hut without facilities. She supported herself by giving English lessons. She went daily to market for food, except when she came to bake marvelous apple pies in the Casady oven.

Another day, Virginia and I visited a small ranch where a man from a U.S. university was developing new apple varieties. How I wish the truly sensational apple I tasted there would show up here! Another day we spent shopping for colorful Guatemala fabrics. It happened that this was the week of a fair in which booths from different areas showed their own distinctive woven designs. We spent one day in a village watching weavers work and visiting one for tea inside her hut. Virginia communicated well.

One summer, I helped John and his brother Phil remodel Mom's home as a surprise while she was spending a month in Annapolis with her other son George. As I said in the Robin, "It would drive us crazy to do it while she was here; she is so confused and changeable. She complains over and over about the uneven floors, and the dreariness of the place. We know she will be pleased with her new carpet all through the house, including the kitchen and the bath. Judy and I tramped all over town to find draperies to go with the "ginger spice" color of the carpet. Phil is helping John paint the walls, the cabinets, and later the outside of the house. I have washed all her dishes, pans, etc. (which were in very bad shape, poor dear)." In another excerpt, I say that:

> She is getting steadily more difficult to live with—not that she's in our house, but she gets phoning jags, calling us six or more times in an evening about the most preposterous things. She is obsessed with the fear that some of her "treasures" will go to someone outside the family. I can feel compassion for her, but it bugs me that she can think of nothing else to leave us of herself except material things. It hurts her that we don't leap at the chance

to inherit her old stuff. Even a box of old ribbons and rags will occasion an urgent call asking us to come over right now, she has some important business to take up with us!

We try to prevent the incessant jangling of the phone some nights when we come home especially tired, by taking the phone off the hook as both John and I have to talk with people all day. But that doesn't work, for she will come over with her walker in the dark if the line is busy! I wonder if I will get that attached to material things in my old age. God forbid!

Not much changed when she returned from Annapolis. She liked the way we improved her place well enough. We hired a college girl to come every day to fix her supper and spend the night, but Mom complained constantly about Terri, though she was a particularly lucky "find." It was sad that mom's personality had changed so much that we nearly forgot how vigorous, loving, and helpful to the kids she had been during earlier years.

A few months later, she had a small stroke and broke some ribs. After healing in a convalescent hospital, she was moved into "TLC" (Tender Loving Care), the best of four permanent care facilities we were able to find. John or I went to TLC to see her every day or so. When she was able, we took her for a ride. Other family members often visited her. She got around well on her walker and I'm sure was more contented there than she had been at home.

She adjusted well until four years later when she fell and broke a vertebra. She would no longer be able to leave her bed. It was awful to see her in pain. She would grip our hands tightly as long as we stayed. When pain pills by mouth didn't give her enough relief, the doctor finally gave her injections despite the danger that they might suppress her breathing. However, it was agreed that pain relief was the most important consideration now. She seemed to be resting peacefully then, but she didn't live long after that. We got the clan together after her death and had a simple funeral to share memories of her early days and look at pictures.

Now there was too much land and too big a house for John and me. We dreamed of developing our two remaining acres into a circle of cottages around a landscaped area featuring a little waterfall flowing from that huge outcropping of rocks. On the summer before my sabbatical,

I began investigating whether this plan was realistic. Condominiums were just becoming popular. I had seen in El Cajon a group of beautiful small homes surrounded by trees. I learned that this was a "PRD" (planned residential development) when I talked to a man at the city's planning department. He and another man came to see what I had in mind. They encouraged the project as we sat around the picnic table and discussed how to proceed with the plan.

First I would need to have the land surveyed, including the topography, then to employ a firm of engineers to draw specific plans and then to see a bank about financing the project. As I look back, I can't imagine why I hadn't been too overwhelmed to go ahead, but I did. I spent much time and several thousand dollars to have the survey done. I found a company to work with me in drawing plans for the cottages and their placement around the landscaped circle.

Now comes one of those coincidences that often make such a difference in life. I had a hobby of studying floor plans and imagining how our family would live in these plans, so I was all ready to go with a floor plan for the cottages. (John and I would be living in one!) My helper said, "Hmm, yes that looks good; I've seen trailers with plans like that."

"What?" I said, "Do they make trailers that big?" I hadn't heard of "mobile homes" or manufactured housing at that time. I remembered only the single-wide trailer at Lake Henshaw that Donna and Wayne had lived in the first summer of their marriage.

"Where could I see one of those things?" I asked.

"Oh, there are several companies along Main Street. You can't miss finding one."

"And where do people put them?"

"Well, our company has been designing Pecan Park a few miles east, along the freeway. The owner urged us to save as many trees as possible as we design the lot placement."

I was intrigued by the discovery that there were already small cottage-like structures that could be placed in attractive surroundings with trees like Pecan Park. That night John and I saw our first mobile home and approved it with enthusiasm. What ingenious use of space! How well designed and attractive!

The next day I visited the construction site of Pecan Park. Someone there mentioned another park on the other side of the freeway. I remembered my newspaper clipping about a controversy when a company applied for a permit to create a "trailer park" close to the shores of Lake Jennings. I had deplored the idea! Now I drove over to have a look.

I talked with the agent stationed at the entrance. I let him believe I might be interested in reserving a space. He drove me around to see what was available. He warned me that the most attractive lots were going fast. I could reserve one for $100, which would be refunded if my home didn't sell after three months. (I hadn't even thought about selling it!)

That night when John came home, I met him with this: "You can't believe what I did today! I wrote a check for $100 for a mobile-home space, just in case. It's for one of the few lots with a good view of Lake Jennings and El Capitan Mountain. The $100 is refundable, though." He was not too shocked. We had already begun to realize that the cost of developing our land and building the cottages would make them so expensive that people would probably choose mobile homes. My session with the bank had not been encouraging.

When we drove out toward Lake Jennings and saw the park's layout close to the mountain, John was as pleased as I with the idea of life there away from the city. Even so, we dawdled. Should we do it? Do we really want to leave our beloved home full of memories and surrounded by trees that had grown up with our family? And how would we go about selling it?

Just then came another life-changing coincidence. At this very time our nephew Doug Bosco happened to be in the area for a short time and was staying with us. He spent one evening with Donna and Wayne in their almost-new tract home in Santee. They were busily planting trees and decorating the interior. The next morning at breakfast, I could hardly believe it when Doug mentioned a casual remark that had been made at dinner the previous night with the Gruenewald family. They wished they could afford to buy the old home place. What! How could they prefer this ragged house and land to their brand new up-to-date place?

The answer was in their warm memories of family gatherings they had enjoyed here: Thanksgiving dinners, birthday parties, picnics.

This place had "stayed put" while they had moved again and again to unfamiliar environments. They hated seeing the family home go to strangers.

By the time we checked to see if they were really interested in living there, I had figured out how we could make it happen. It worked. We did it. We sold them half interest in the place. They sold the Santee house; with mortgage funds, they paid us for our half. We calculated the price by getting a professional assessment and averaging it with the assessment on the property-tax bill.

I went to see my friend Harry Riley in his mobile home. It was beautiful and tastefully furnished by his new wife. (His first wife Marsha, a close friend of mine, had died of cancer several years before.) The company from whom Harry had bought his house would build to customers' specifications. John and I studied their wide variety of options, paid for our selection with the Gruenewald money, and moved to Space /3 in February 1972.

We had plenty of time to bring belongings to our numerous cabinets, drawers, and closets. I brought important items first, planning to discard any leftovers when spaces were filled. It turned out that our new home had more storage space than the old one.

At my friend Audrey's, I had seen and loved the work of John Mumford, who called himself a landscape artist. He was delighted to work with us and obliterate any of the tinny look of old-fashioned trailers. Instead of the usual siding and skirting, we had dark green, rough-textured Masonite woody walls. Our "artist" joined the walls to the skirting, making it look more like what was then called a "stick-built" house.

We aimed for a mountain cabin appearance with details like those I had gleaned from my Japanese garden books. Mumford made an elaborate design with an abundance of plants and liquidambar trees—too many as time went on. He brought in soil and truckloads of huge rocks. He had his workers construct an ornamental pool connected to a simulated spring with bubbling water and a circulating motor. To make his colored cement for sidewalks look like quarry rock, he threw plastic-shielded rocks on it.

He built the porch and carport, using enough redwood to cover metal where appropriate. All this made his work almost as expensive as the house itself, but it was great fun and was joyful for years as the plants grew. The trees reminded us of the maples we liked in Ohio, especially when they displayed brilliant autumn colors and when they sprouted the first pale green signs of spring.

Ironically, when I was teaching at El Cap in Lakeside, I drove to work from El Cajon. Then I transferred to Valhalla in El Cajon and drove the other way. Because our house was close to the freeway, it didn't take much extra time for either John or me.

I have lived in this house longer than in any other. First there was the farm where I was born, then the little house at the edge of McComb until high school graduation. Then we had the Toledo years, first with John's parents, then the attic apartment above the Mannones, and the new house on Pasadena Blvd. Then we came to the ranch in California where we lived twenty-six years. Now, as I write this, I have spent exactly twenty-six years here at Lake Jennings!

This park is for older people: at least one in each house must be 55 or older. I was 55 when we moved in; John was 59. It was a perfect place to retire. Aside from the great view of mountains and the lake and green out of every window, we appreciate the feeling of safety. Neighbors are congenial and helpful in case of emergency; the fire station and paramedics are less than a mile away.

Six years after we moved here, we both retired and started another chapter of our lives while we enjoyed watching the varied life stories of our offspring.

Tim's life was the most dramatic. Ups and downs with Jeanine alternated with lifestyle decisions. He met and coupled with Jeanine shortly after returning from submarine duty. They vacillated for a while over whether to marry. Jeanine's broken family made her skeptical of the institution of marriage. Tim seemed to require more independence and solitude than an everyday relationship can provide. One summer, he and his cousin Michael traveled around the country in their improvised live-in old van.

When Tim and Jeanine did marry, they lived for a short time in our tent trailer on the ranch and then on their land on Honey Springs Road about twenty-five miles away. They bought ten acres of hillside on the lower slope of Lyons Peak with plans to build a house there. It had a beautiful wide view, a flowing stream, and many rocks, which Tim moved about with an unbelievable exertion of energy and determination. He dreamed of building a house with all known ways of using sunlight for economy and comfort.

He started digging a well, expecting to finish it, a septic tank, and a shelter by fall! At the same time, he was working forty hours a week at Golden Arrow. But I said in the Robin that

> I've never seen him healthier or happier. He is just crazy about figuring out how to do difficult projects—this well, for example. He has to line it with concrete down to twenty feet. He figured out that he would make the forms with lumber that would later be usable for the house. He arranged ropes to haul buckets of soil to the surface.
>
> Yesterday I was talking with Jeanine about this well, how scary it was to look down into it and not even see the bottom—all the "what ifs"—and I asked, "Wouldn't it be cheaper to have the well drilled like everybody else does?" She laughed and said, "He just likes to dig!"
>
> Remember how kids want to dig to China? Perhaps Tim is still pretty much of a kid. And then sometimes he reminds me of Daddy, who was so inventive, doing things a bit differently from the conventional way. If only Daddy were here now to kibbitz with Tim about this project. All he has to go on is a one-page diagram from the health department, and they had to hunt for that. They said nobody had dug a well for ages. Not even the government printing office had anything to send him. He has already dug below the depth his extension ladder will reach. I've got to quit writing about this. My dreams are bad enough as it is!

By fall he had been told that he couldn't continue living in the trailer. The county gave him a sixty-day notice, so he hurried to get a tiny "tool shed" up before the deadline. This became an amazing structure. The tiny entry did have space for tools, but the rest, below the size that would require a permit, became a livable split-level home for one person. He constructed a bed space above the tools, with a window that opened to let the cat in. The main area became a kitchen, complete with bottled gas, cooking plate, and sink. I don't believe there was a law against living in a tool shed!

Meanwhile, the well had reached the depth of twenty feet. He was required to line it that far with cement. As I told the Robin readers:

Tim is still waiting around for permission to go ahead with his road so he can have access to his well for cement delivery. He's getting disgusted with bureaucracy, even though he is part of it himself. As you know, after a short stint at the dairy, he now works for the city of El Cajon as a maintenance man.

Alas, the rainy season came before he was able to get that cement in and applied. Only half of what I had been fearing came to pass. When rain dissolved the walls of the well, it caved in. Thankfully, Tim was not in it!

Jeanine rented a tiny house in La Mesa. It was her plan to give piano lessons. Her grand piano filled the living room. She went to Los Angeles once a week for lessons. She was an accomplished player of concert music, having won a contest for a musical scholarship. She planned to enter some competitions. She and I were as close as I was with my other daughters. She gave me piano lessons and persuaded me to buy a new Yamaha to replace my hundred-dollar antique.

I was convinced that it had to go, even though I loved its Victorian decoration and its nice wood. Years before, John had spent hours on the Anza porch sanding the crusty surface it had developed through the years. He stained it and polished it to a nice glow. Happily, an impersonal secondhand store wasn't the buyer. A woman who did buy it liked it as I did. Her children were to begin piano lessons. I love it when my discards find happy homes.

A while later, Jeanine went to a college in Nebraska and earned a Masters degree. When she returned, she bought a house and we all kept in contact for a number of years, but the marriage ended in divorce and we gradually lost touch.

# RETIREMENT BEGINS

As I start this chapter, I realize that the period of retirement is a third of my life. Despite some difficulties, these years have been filled with rewarding experiences. John and I have enjoyed traveling between periods of rough going with health problems. Our children have been living good lives. We have had all the money we needed or wanted and we have both been content in our final home.

I helped to maintain this contentment when I participated in Lake Jennings's legal committee and the board. A retired lawyer, Richard Adams, started our confrontation with the park owner when he announced a greatly increased space rent, despite his assurance when we rented our lots that any increased cost would be no more than would be justified by increased expenses of utilities and maintenance.

Because we had no such guarantee in writing, residents assumed we couldn't do anything about it. Dick, however, said that if enough of us were willing to go to court and testify to the verbal guarantee, we could prevail. We did go to court. We were successful. Years of further activity kept alive this contest between resident and owner rights.

Probably the most dramatic incident in this story took place when Dick and Irene Adams came home from a meeting to find their house in flames. It was definitely arson. Without evidence of the perpetrator, there was no conviction.

When we few litigants in the first court case not only won but were awarded monetary damages, most other residents were willing to join us in further actions. The jury awarded damages to plaintiffs against the owners for "loss in value of home, punitive damages, and emotional distress"—a total of $28,500 for John and me. When I had been testifying, a lawyer asked me whether this situation had affected me emotionally. I said, "Not especially except when Mr. Adams's house was burned down. That worried me because I had been on the legal committee." I'm not sure whether that arson had been previously mentioned.

Later on, we residents formed a corporation and bought the park. After many ups and downs, the corporation became a condominium and most of us now own the land beneath our houses.

For three years, I chaired a study group in the League of Women Voters after a warm-up conference in San Francisco. The first year, 1983, we studied and prepared programs for unit meetings on the subject of national security. With different League members the second year, our topic was arms control. The third year, we studied the third world. We planned a large program for the membership of both the AAUW and the LWV entitled "What About Russia?" Speakers were an analyst from the San Diego newspaper, a history professor, and an experienced visitor to Russia who showed slides along with his comments.

John supported me when I was engaged in the park's legal activities and in the League of Women Voters. He participated in Great Decisions discussions. However, he had his own continuing interests, mainly golf and painting. Years before, he happened to say he wished he could paint pictures, not just the house. So one Christmas the kids bought him a kit of materials to get him started, but he never had time to use them—until now.

He joined a painting class where they made oil paintings of pictures they liked. His modified versions of these scenes were more beautiful than the originals. He was skillful at creating subtle colors of the sky, mountains, and trees. He spent hours on one large painting, dabbing at rocks to get them just right. There were so many rocks! His work still hangs on walls here and in the homes of our relatives.

Still another life-changing coincidence happened when John stayed overnight in the hospital after cataract surgery—the custom in those days. His roommate with the same surgery, Lawrence (Larry) Brullo, taught classes in watercolor painting. When I came to take John home,

Larry's wife, a teacher, was also there. She was discussing plans to take Larry home during her lunch hour.

"Oh, let us take him home! You don't live far from us," we offered. Larry's daughter was amused when she met us at the door, her dad with a big patch on his right eye, John with a big patch on the left. We went in, chatted, and had breakfast, and then admired Larry's watercolor paintings. John forever stopped that tedious painting of rocks with oil and enrolled in Larry's watercolor class.

In summer, the class sometimes went to Italy to paint. Larry, of Italian descent, knew the country and enough of the language to arrange perfect trips. In October 1982, John and I joined the group. For two weeks, the watercolor painters worked on scenes of our small town, Pienza. We spouses and others visited a half dozen beautiful hill towns in Tuscany. Our bus driver had driven us north from Rome and stayed with us. Sometimes the artists took the day off and went with us. One day, I took a long walk along a country road admiring the unspoiled open spaces around Pienza, where housing used so little space but managed to be attractive and always neat. Every day was a joy for me.

The whole group had dinner together around a long table. Painters shared their day's work. We admired; Larry made suggestions. I am reminded of this delightful two weeks when I see John's paintings, framed and hanging above our living room sofa.

Another year, John went with Larry's group to Sicily. Both he and I were perfectly content with our way of pursuing our separate interests and at the same time doing things together: trips and long morning walks and games at home. Here's how I described our life in the Robin:

> Retirement is nice, though the time seems to go faster than ever. John and I are both unbelievably lazy. I am ashamed that we spend so much time in front of the TV. He likes all the ball games and some of the game shows, both of which I dislike. Fortunately, we have an extra TV in the bedroom, so when he's watching in there, I can play the piano to my heart's content without disturbing him.

> We both accepted a request to serve on a committee to select AFS candidates. The American Field Service operates a program of exchanging students with other countries. High school kids

apply; then we pick the ones we think would benefit most from a year in another land. I have had several students from other countries in my classes through the years. They usually speak English after a fashion, but many of our kids go over without the slightest familiarity with the language of the host country. Amazingly, they do pick up a working knowledge of it after three or four months. Our Karl thinks he might apply.

Karl never went, but a few years later, the Gruenewalds were hosts to Rana from Jordan. They all did so well together that Rana came back and stayed until she finished college and met her future husband Luay before going home. She called me "Grandma." I met her mother and father when they visited here. Rana kept in touch for years, sending pictures of her home and children.

In 1979, the year after we retired, John and I took our first long trip in our Toyota Chinook, a magically designed miniature motor home. Though it was no longer than our Ford, it had a fridge, bottled-gas stove, sink, storage space, and a porta-potty. The bench and table could be quickly reassembled to make a double bed. It was perfect for us. It took little gas (23 mpg) and was easy to drive and park, making it work well as a second car. Many years later when John was no longer able to drive and we no longer needed two cars, we sold it to my sister Edna and her husband. Carl enjoyed refurbishing it; they used it for years.

Before starting our cross-country trip, we resolved to drive at 55 miles an hour, the legal limit at the time. We were in no hurry to reach a particular destination but wanted to fully enjoy the country. We passed only three cars the whole trip. Everyone passed us, especially the wildly speeding trucks.

We planned the trip around state park campgrounds and homes of relatives. In Bartlesville, Oklahoma, we spent a couple days with my cousin Donald Smith just as he was about to retire from his position with Phillips Petroleum. He took us on a tour of the lab facilities he had been overseeing. We went through room after room of awesome setups of sophisticated equipment designed to analyze oil samples and relay findings to decision makers via an up-to-date computer.

The company had just finished an enormous building with tastefully finished offices. Workers were hanging walls with original paintings of famous artists. One wing of the building displayed many products made from oil or with its use. It seems inappropriate that huge planting boxes and other plastics using oil are pushed for sale at a time when oil resources are known to be finite, leaving us still not ready with alternate ways of getting around. Donald showed us a chart that showed that we have already used up 75% of available supplies. That is scary when you realize that we have been using oil for only a short time and that the bulk of this consumption has taken place since World War II.

Donald's wife Ruth collects and renews antique furniture. In a few months they will move to their farm nearby where their garden is already, in late May, producing lettuce, onions, and radishes. They plan to live in a small house on the property while they build a larger one using their plan for central heating based on a huge recirculating fireplace, which will be surrounded with beautiful walnut or other fine hardwood. Ruth has been collecting hardwoods for years. They will be used throughout the house for walls and window frames.

We enjoyed two days in Lake of the Ozarks and three with David's family. Then we spent a week and a half with Mother along with side trips to Bluffton College and the Toledo relatives. After we went out to dinner with Keith and Frances Barkimer, we saw their shop, where they sold turquoise jewelry and other Indian artworks, which they bought directly from Indians of the Southwest. Years later, they continued this interest in Albuquerque, New Mexico. When we visited them there, Keith introduced us to artistic pottery workers. They made us an earthenware chandelier with our choice of colors and shapes. It hangs above our dining table.

We found Jeanine's father in Beaver, Pennsylvania, in spite of an intricate system of weird turns and bottlenecks. The street pattern was not built with heavy auto traffic in mind. Beaver is a lovely old town with towering trees. We visited Jeanine's sister Janey and her daughter Jonalynn. Janey worked in a serene library along a quiet river.

The Gettysburg battlefield brought me memories of Daddy looking it over when I was about nine. Mother, Irene, and both grandmothers were on that trip. I read a few markers on this vaguely familiar battlefield, but found the subject of battles boring. My interest in history still doesn't extend very far toward how battles are won or lost, but how they can be prevented.

Next stop: Annapolis, where we visited John's oldest brother George, his wife Baynie, and his son Jack. George had retired from the Maryland Hall of Records but was still doing part time work for them. He had previously been senate librarian.

We went into Washington for two days. We were fascinated by the subway system, which we experienced for the first time. We also admired the shuttle bus as it took us to a science building and the Smithsonian where we spent much time going through art galleries. Senator Cranston's office gave us tickets to visit the Senate and the House. In a letter to Mother, I observed that "the House of Representatives was at least twice as unruly as any classroom I have ever presided over. The chairman insisted on quiet every few minutes, to no avail. He pleaded with them to go out into the halls if they wanted to talk, but they were soon whooping it up again."

Then we drove north to Ipswich to see my cousin Harold. He took us on a tour through quaint shops, art galleries, and fish markets where you could have a live lobster cooked to order. We walked along the harbor, where we took pictures of stacks of lobster traps, sailboats, and picturesque old barns. He took us out to dinner in a historic house being used as a restaurant. Many houses are marked with their ages—in the 1600's—and protected by law from being changed on the outside.

Harold told us of his days as an Air Force test pilot and of his experience in the meatpacking business. He was now president of a community college in Boston. He told us he spent a summer as a prison guard in preparation for writing curriculum for guards. This was subsequently used by New York officials at all prisons except the one at Attica where that awful riot killed so many. He told us all about his journey to Taiwan where he shared his knowledge about how to develop a community college.

All the way across the country, I had practiced my French with tapes, hoping I could communicate with people when we reached Montreal. Not so, alas! Though I was delighted to hear children and everyone else speaking it lickety-split in the ultra-nice KOA campground, I understood none of it, except for one short conversation I had in the swimming pool with a bilingual woman.

The trip across the trans-Canada freeway was uneventful. The Lake Louise area was lovely: the road north was glorious, with towering mountains, mirror lakes, breathtaking vistas on all sides. In Jasper, we took a tram to the top of a mountain where we hiked and warmed with tea and muffins. On the way back south, we tried to locate the place where my parents and I had stayed back in 1929. No such luck: slightly familiar but more built up.

A day in a Vancouver park; another in Portland with John's cousin Mary Emma; four with Mary, Edna and company—especially Caroll's babies—in Sebastopol and Novato; a stop to see niece Robin's new baby girl; then home! After six weeks.

When the Vietnam conflict was growing increasingly worrisome in the sixties, we teachers sometimes discussed it briefly. I felt that America's actions there were mistaken. Wondering what the government's rationale could be, I invited for an evening of discussion a few friends—a fellow teacher and two State College professors I knew who might be able to explain it. Instead of explaining the reasons for the war, however, they too, agreed that it was not justified!

That led to years of Great Decisions discussion groups, off and on until I retired. Then I joined the AAUW, American Association of University Women, to get another group together. When some husbands expressed interest, I formed an evening group. Members bought a yearly booklet produced by the Foreign Policy Association, containing background material on eight significant issues in U.S. foreign policy.

From 1980 to 1999, about forty people attended the group meetings, about a dozen regularly. After an interlude due to health problems, several former Great Decisions members urged me to restart the meetings. I corralled a new group to meet once a month in my home to study, commiserate about present catastrophes, consider what should be done, and weigh the advantages and disadvantages of proposed policies.

In 1984, I volunteered to help Jim Skelly and Chuck Nathanson, who were involved in attempts to establish a U.S. Institute of Peace. First, I organized and annotated their piles of clippings. Then I audited their course "Nuclear Weapons and American Society" at UCSD. For Chuck, I often went to the university library to locate and check out books.

In my final volunteer job at the university, I worked for IGCC, the Institute on Global Conflict and Cooperation. I was invited to join the faculty at luncheon seminars with foreign policy speakers. My first task with Helen Hawkins was working in the office of Roger Revelle's secretary to type cards for the Institute's book collection. Then Helen, who was editing a biography of Leo Szilard, taught me to use the computer so I could help her by sorting and writing short annotations of letters written to and by Szilard on the subject of taming the atomic bomb. He had been one of the scientists most responsible for starting the atom bomb project during WWII when it was learned that Germany was trying to develop such a weapon. He and others tried unsuccessfully to stop work on this defensive horror after Germany was defeated and it was therefore no longer needed, they believed.

Feeling compelled to do what they could to tame its power, they decided to focus on the U.S. Senate. They founded the "Council for a Livable World." Originally, the letterhead of this organization said "To Eliminate Nuclear Weapons." Later it became "To Eliminate Weapons of Mass Destruction." Before elections, candidates most likely to advance this goal are described on two-sided pages with their qualifications and the odds of their winning. We members are asked to send contributions directly to campaigns of candidates the council prefers. We have been reasonably successful. I was invited to a luncheon that the CLW officers held at the university. Their advice is always worth considering, though I don't always agree with the lawmakers they recommend.

My only remaining volunteer activity is leading the Great Decisions study group monthly in my home, where we share concerns over an increasingly dangerous world and our hopes that ways can be developed to save our children from disastrous conflict.

# OVERSEAS AND ELDERHOSTELS

Two women I knew, one a counselor at Valhalla, the other a friend of Mary Jane, each told me about their trips to London. June's story sounded so similar to Grace's, that I decided they should meet each other. I planned a get-together with them and other friends who heard about it and asked to be included. We had so much to talk about that this group of eight or so met every month for a long while, in a different restaurant each time.

Both June and Grace had gone alone to London and stayed in an inexpensive hotel run by the Salvation Army. They gave me pamphlets, maps, brochures, inspiration—and courage to follow in their footsteps. A booklet from the Holiday Fellowship offered a wide variety of holiday weeks throughout England and Scotland. Walking as a main theme was coupled with other themes like golf, arts, historical buildings, beginning tennis, or advanced bridge. A program not far from London for older walkers caught my eye.

Before I made a reservation, I happened to be in Ohio and went to see Mary Morrison Johnston, who had recently lost her husband to cancer. She and I had been together in school since the second grade and in Campfire Girls. As we got up-to-date on our lives, I learned that her family, like mine, had been active hikers and campers. Her children, like mine, were now on their own. Inspiration struck. "Say, Mary, I'm planning a hiking trip to England next summer. How about going along?"

"Tell me more," she said. "I've been planning to spend several weeks with Tom in Germany. Maybe I could do another week in England." Mary's son heads the Amerikahaus in Hanover, the information arm of the American embassy.

Toward the end of July, I visited Mother and Webster in Ohio, then met Mary in New York. We flew to London together and took a bus to Sunnydown, close to the southern coast. We spent a week in an old stone cottage with nine other guests, the host, his wife, and their daughter. In a letter to Mother, I describe the week:

I couldn't sleep on the plane going over, so I kept nodding off that first night when our host showed his fine slides. I slunk off to bed the first possible moment. Next morning, naturally, I wakened at the crack of dawn—5:30—though we weren't supposed to make any noise until 7:30. Torture! The steps creaked in the old house and the walls were thin.

Fortunately, Nora wakened by and by. She and I took a walk down to the crossroad from which we got a view of the ocean and Corfe Castle, an ancient ruin that gives its name to a quaint village. Nora spends fifty weeks a year caring for her elderly invalid mother. One of her two weeks off she spends with her daughter, the other she is spending in Sunnydown.

Hilda is a very special lady, a Quaker. She walks with a cane and didn't go on our regular hikes with us, though she did go slowly down to a nearby village when the rest of us were off somewhere else. I saw glimpses of pain in her eyes from time to time. We talked together of the nuclear threat and British politics. (She's hopeful the new party will succeed.) She is active in peace movements. We shared addresses.

Elsie, 70, was full of vigor and spunk. After divorcing a husband who beat her, she went to work for an American who had started a school in Switzerland for American young people learning European languages, customs, etc. Elsie's job was to guide them to cultural spots and try to smooth off the rough edges of their manners.

After she explained to us the difficulty of training them to eat "properly" with their knives permanently in their right hands, forks in the left, I found it rather uncomfortable to eat at her table!

I did practice eating right, and quickly weaned myself from coffee and took to having tea with milk as they do.

On one hike, it grew very hot, so Elsie simply peeled off her blouse and walked along in her bra with complete lack of embarrassment. Like many of our hikes, though, this one was out in the country with no one around but half dozen women. We often walked along fence rows in fields privately owned.

Easements for hikers are a long tradition in England, but during the war when all land possible had to be cultivated, farmers were pleased to take over this hiking space. Then after the war was over, they tried to prevent resumption of the hiking easements. Well! Spunky little Elsie was not about to let that happen. She helped start an organization, ran for a town council and won, serving for several years. They got the easements back.

Hikers are supposed to stay within so many feet of the fence and make sure gates are closed. Usually there are quite a few brambles and not much of a path, but it's a wonderful way to see the country.

Joy was a scatterbrained, talkative woman. Alexandra was tall, classy, well organized. George and Etta, the only couple, were genial and dignified. I enjoyed Scrabble with them and conversation with them and most of the others.

Wilfred was such an odd character I've saved him for last. Small, nervous, wearing dark-rimmed glasses, he introduced himself by announcing that he is diabetic, pointing to a badge and to his pocket where we could find some candy to get out for him if he seemed to be slipping into a diabetic coma. We saw no signs whatever of physical distress during the week, but the poor man was in a constant tizzy for fear he would not be in the right place at the right time so he could eat on schedule. After a sojourn, he would sprint to be first to the bathroom so he could take his blood or urine sample.

He made quite a to-do in the kitchen about his diet and discussed the matter to the point of obsession. Although he worried about the excess of carbohydrates over protein in our sack lunches, he served himself five or six times from the plate of cookies that were served in the parlor at bedtime. His condition was his only mark of distinction. As we learned more about him, my pity grew, for he had been a schoolmaster of a group of grade-school boys. It's painful to imagine the torture this Dickensian character must have endured.

Our host, Buck, was a rather young, fat, jolly fellow with vast stores of information about plants, animals, rocks, birds. He told us amazing stories and history and took us to fascinating places. At the beach in Swanage, a row of six cottages are rented for the day to vacationers for changing in, taking a shady nap, or making tea on a hot plate. In the evening, lights went on in the lighthouse as we watched a lovely flock of birds, "kittiwakes," with their young learning to venture out from their Cliffside nests.

The cave, a few feet inland from the cliffs, is called the "Tilly Whim." Names are a delight all over England. Small rivers are "Piddle" and piddle means just what you think. Some places with "puddle" in their names had been "piddle" before the straight-laced Queen Victoria held sway. We saw "carryfast" shops and "Give Way" for yield on road signs. Drug stores are "chemists."

One day, Buck took us to Dorchester along narrow roads lined with high walls of living green. Thatched roofs were the norm. They look like bangs cut low with cutouts for "eyes." They are expensive to keep up, for they require skilled craftsmen to install and repair them, and they are a fire problem. Ironically, in the olden days they were fashionable for the opposite reason: they were the only cheap roofing material.

We saw Thomas Hardy's birthplace and numerous locales described in his novels. A museum named for him is most fascinating. I recall especially some fine paintings, exquisitely detailed baby clothes and other needlework, some natural history displays, and two exhibits done by architects and city planners illustrating tasteful ways to remodel business facades and signs, plus ways to improve the look of a small city by skillfully placed shrubbery and trees. A similar model showed how to make low-cost housing beautiful. How splendid to pay attention to these places, not just private homes for the wealthy few!

I was treated to a highlight of the week upon my arrival when I was given a letter from Barbara, a friend of June's, inviting me to a concert of medieval music in a lovely old church. She had driven several hours to Swanage to visit her cousin "Bill" Bayly and especially to meet me. How heart warming!

I had gone to a similar concert with David in Indiana, but the atmosphere of the ancient church gave this kind of music additional authenticity and superb sound. The talented musicians were on tour. Their instruments were like the pre-1700 hurdy-gurdy, the shawn, the double-reeded ancestor of the oboe. After the concert, we had a late supper at Bayly's apartment. He paints in watercolors and teaches. I asked him to recommend a good watercolor book for beginners. He did. After a great deal of searching when I was back in London, I finally found it and sent it home to John.

One of our daily walks took us up a hill overlooking a saucer-shaped valley containing a manor house with its extra buildings and a small village. All this land and the manor belong to one family, generation after generation. We descended to the village and entered through the "kissing gate," a novel turnstile arrangement.

The village was quiet, serene and beautiful with the local Purbeck marble used for walls and structures. We had tea, bought postcards, and visited a tiny old church with graves alongside, all old and lichen-covered. Inside, the church was fragrant with more than a dozen flower arrangements left from celebrating the previous week's royal wedding.

I loved the churches, every one with its own special feel. One had unique windows. The original ones had been destroyed during the World War II bombing. Instead of replacing them with imitations of the originals, a gifted artist created engraved or etched windows without any color at all, just delicate sprays of flower shapes, diamonds, stars, etc. I could imagine the sun coming through them on a Sunday morning and flooding the place with rainbows, the engravings acting as fanciful prisms. In Wareham, one church had only fourteen chairs and a very old painted list of the Ten Commandments on the wall, nearly faded away. It had been put there during the Norman period, many centuries ago.

The other holiday week I chose was in Scotland. I was to take a bus to the train. It would be a long day's ride north so I had to leave before anyone was up except Buck, who was good enough to take my bag out to the bus stop. I found the train ride north shortened by visiting with a Cleveland woman who was hurrying to be with her mother before she died of cancer. This woman's husband had been fired from his job as a meat inspector in Ohio, she said, when someone in the Reagan administration found him too diligent in weeding out diseased cattle.

I had an adventure in Glasgow where I was to change trains. I was supposed to phone ahead for transportation from the train station. I planned to do that during the thirty-five minutes between trains. But half of the dozen phones were out of order; those that worked had queues in front of them. I had to go buy something to get change and I had a terrible time trying to figure out the phone system when I finally did get one. It rang but there was no answer. I suddenly realized that the time was passing, so I gave up and rushed to the train, just in time to see it pulling out.

This was Saturday. There was no other train until Monday, I learned, but there was a Sunday bus. The bus station and tourist information center were closed. A kind policeman pointed toward the street a couple of blocks away where I could get a bus headed toward the less expensive hotels. What a long two blocks that was! Feeling a bit upset and weary by this time, I stopped and had supper halfway to the bus street. The super-slow service was a blessing: I welcomed a long sit before venturing further into an alien world.

The bus let me off in the dingy section the officer had told me about. (It was no dingier than the rest of Glasgow.) I settled on a hotel with the comforting name of Smith. The manager had no bus schedules; no one answered the bus phone. I worried all night that it would leave before I got there. Fortunately, the next morning a friendly American woman joined me at the breakfast table. (Funny how everyone knows right away if you are American.)

When I told her of my plight, she said, "Oh, I have a bus schedule up in my room." I learned the bus would leave in twenty minutes. I asked the manager to phone a cab for me, packed fast, slapped bacon into a slice of bread and made it! Ah well, one has to have one bad experience to add a little cayenne to the delicious stew of good stuff.

More than a hundred guests were at the hotel on the edge of Loch Awe in Scotland. Except for three young persons from France, eight Germans, and me, they were all English. Three grades of hikes a day were called "A or A-, B+ or B-, or C." I always took the "C" hikes, which were quite strenuous enough for me. In fact, two days I stayed at the hotel to baby my troublesome ankle and to let my boots dry out from the constant drizzly rain. The "drying" room was more like a steam room, always full. The mornings I stayed in gave me a chance to play the piano without anyone around. Evenings were filled with activities, singing, games, and amateur programs. I played the piano.

Excursions here were quite a contrast to those in southern England. Intimate beauty was replaced by magnificent mountain vistas, marshy stretches of heather ,and endless miles of deep blue-green hills. The "C" group, which was usually the largest, rode to our hiking destination in a bus. One day we shopped in Oden, where I bought some fine woolens at low cost. I sent John a pullover and a cardigan. My roommate was a fat, white-haired but youngish lady, congenial but not interesting.

Breakfast was porridge, bacon or sausage, and eggs. We filled sack lunches with our choice of any five items from a big table and a smaller sack with two cookies for afternoon tea. Supper was soup, meat, two cooked vegetables, potatoes, and dessert.

On the train back to London I sat in a section opposite "Mum" and Dad and their fourteen-year-old Graham, returning from the Glasgow wedding of their daughter. Poor Graham had to take a lot of guff from his father, who made him toe the mark. Secretly, I cheered him on when he was justifiably fresh with the old man, who would put up with no sign of "greediness" or insubordination from the kid but who sneaked several cigarettes under the "No Smoking! £50 Penalty" sign and did away with a couple cans of Extra Stout Ale and more than his share of goodies.

I arrived at Vandon House at 5:00, in time to explore immediate surroundings and go to the nearby grocery to buy some yogurt, peanuts, and cookies to supplement the bacon/tomato sandwich I had had on the train. My 7' by 12' room was close to a nearby toilet and bath. I had breakfast next morning with a woman from Tasmania, and then was off to an early start. I stopped for a tube of Lanacane and to my amazement, the "chemist" invited me to join him in a cup of coffee he was in the process of preparing. I agreed, though I'd already had two cups. He pointed me to a stool in his tiny alchemy alcove. "Adlai" and I compared life histories. He came from Egypt, and had worked for the BBC. After three interruptions for other customers, I bought my Lanacane, film, and toothpaste and moved on.

The next adventure of the day was at Hyde Park speakers' corner to hear a socialist tell one of his haranguers that because of the capitalist system we can no longer help ourselves to a cave, "though judging from the degree of intelligence you display in your remarks you belong in a cave." Other hecklers were castigated for the "bloody stupidity" of their remarks. All brickbats were verbal; there was never the slightest feeling that anyone would start using fists—or worse.

I took the two-hour Round London tour for $2.50 and a walking tour called "Upstairs/Downstairs" in the upscale Belgravia section of expensive row houses. Each house had three floors, each with one window, a basement with stairs in front, a metal fence, and a gate at the street. A separate elegant stair led to the main living quarters. All homes were owned by one nobleman who leased them for long periods. He required a uniform paint, Magnolia 232, made by his own company so it would forever be available.

I saw two good plays, *Overheard*, with Deborah Kerr, and *Annie*, with several young actors. There were amusing references to FDR and the depression. The English are fond of good-natured digs at America. On the third day, I braved the underground "tube" to go to the Tower of London. Guides in Beefeater costumes spoke beautiful English to tell us chilling anecdotes about the moat, the gate, and executions.

Twice I visited the National Gallery, where I enjoyed originals of paintings I'd seen only in reproductions: Cezanne landscapes, Renoir, Picasso, and Degas. I passed up an opportunity to see the wedding gifts of Charles and Diana. I happened upon a queue of lookers so long that signs were placed along the line saying "30 minutes to here, 60 … , 90 …", and so on. Imagine being that interested in lavish collections of stuff!

I went to Stratford-on-Avon on a British Shrinkers tour. The guide at Anne Hathaway's home made us feel the life of Shakespearean days.

We saw a fine medieval castle and climbed a high tower via a circular staircase. We shuddered at a dungeon and instruments of torture on a tour of Windsor Castle. In Westminster Abbey on my final morning in London, I appreciated the small room full of "treasures" more than the big famous room packed with tours and their noisy guides.

My sixth and final week was spent in Hanover, Germany, with Mary Johnston and her son Tom. He speaks German well and a few other languages. His staff of six included a librarian. They had U.S. materials for Germans who read English, especially for students doing research. Whether or not Tom always agreed with U.S. policies, he explained them to those who asked. He arranged seminars and forums. When a group of young people occupied the lobby in protest of U.S. nuclear armament policies, the police came in to get them out, but Tom said, "No, as long as they aren't damaging anything, I'll talk with them as long as they want." They finally left peacefully. A letter in the German newspaper praised how well he had handled the situation.

Tom was to go to Moscow the next year and then to China. His wife Rona lived in their apartment in Washington where she was finishing studies for a degree in clinical psychology. They got together just a few times a year. She is Jewish and feels uncomfortable when she comes to Germany. I can imagine how she feels, for I too kept looking about and wondering what this or that older person was doing when the Nazis were in power.

One day, Tom took us to Lubeck, where Thomas Mann lived and wrote. We rode on the Autobahn where cars go about 80 miles an hour. Back in '81 that was frightening, but with everyone going that speed, it seemed almost normal. We visited four churches, the rathaus (government building), and an old hospital where each patient had a kind of tiny house inside a gymnasium-like structure.

We had supper one night in the fine home of a doctor, his wife, their five young children, and two friends, all of whom spoke both languages. The mother was American. In the front yard was a bunker where people had sheltered from bombs during the war. A stream in the large back yard separated it from a vast park with only trees and paths. Many such parks in Germany reminded me of fairy tales.

Sometimes Mary and I went to town on the streetcar half a block away. Cardboard tokens in quantity are bought in advance. You poke them into a slot that marks the time. Even if you get on and off or change cars, the token lets you on until the time is up. There was no conductor. Strips along the sidewalks are set aside for bikes.

The week we were there happened to be the time of the annual festival. Everyone came by streetcar, leaving city space free of cars and available for a riotous variety of activities. For children, there were games like wheeling a wheelbarrow full of balloons, bowling, pedal cars, and an organ grinder with monkeys. There were all kinds of music groups just out of earshot from each other: a symphonic band playing Beethoven's *Fifth*, jazz, rock, spirituals, folk singing. It was fun when everyone joined a singing group. I knew many of the songs; some were Gershwin's. Once they sang a familiar Jewish song with great gusto. I was moved by this. There were dozens of food booths. We shared samples of pizza, cappuccino, doughnuts, "chef's delight," and ouzo. What a combination!

At a flea market, Tom was thrilled to find a wooden antique clock to add to his collection. When someone told Tom that there was going to be a demonstration in front of Amerikahaus, we went there earlier than we had intended to do on our way home. Tom would turn off the lights and make it appear empty. We waited, and when a small crowd with placards and speeches came, we stood on a table and watched through a high window. No problem.

One day, Mary and I followed a self-guided tour through Hanover. Along a painted red line, we'd stop to read what our pamphlet said about numbered points of interest. As we sat on a low wall studying our map, a perky little old lady in a bowler hat stopped and by pointing and gesturing made us understand that she wanted to help us find what we were looking for. "Rathaus," we said. "Ah!" She walked with us three or four blocks while pointing to the paper sack she was carrying and speaking very slowly and distinctly as if that would help us understand her German. She enjoyed cautioning us as we crossed the street.

Shortly, we came to the rathaus and started to cross that street. "Nein! Nein!" She wouldn't have it, she made clear with a torrent of German as she pointed again to her sack and headed toward "Wasser." We thought this meant "water," but we were more and more puzzled as she resisted our crossing over even at the next intersection. We were both baffled, but I said to Mary, "Let's go along with her to see what she has in mind: it might be more interesting than the rathaus," which by now we were leaving behind.

At last we arrived at some "Wasser," a lake. Now for the treat our little lady had for us. She opened her paper bag and gave each of us a bun to throw to the swans, which came up to meet us. We tore and threw until they were all gone. Then our lady dusted off her hands and beckoned toward the traffic light. Now we could go to the rathaus. She walked with us through a grassy path that wound in and out along still another lake. We communicated very well without needing language by pointing out this and that lovely thing. I took a picture of her and Mary with their arms around each other.

Above the rathaus is a tower which we reached by an outside elevator, one of only two in the world which go up at an angle, so as to follow the contour of the dome. The whole city is visible from the top of the tower, and a beautiful city it was. Downstairs we spent a long time examining models of the city, one an ancient version with walls, moats, and one old church, the next as it looked centuries later, five times as large with many churches but with the walls and moats gone.

Number three was similar in size but devastated by the bombing of World War II. After we had spent so much time on the previous model, trying to identify landmarks from the ancient city and marveling at the extent of its progress, this third model affected us like an electric shock. Many of the old landmarks we had traced so carefully were now piles of rubble. Scarcely a roof remained, just a city full of bits of wall.

The final model was the rebuilt city, so completely changed that even in the street patterns we could find scarcely a trace of the old original. One church was undamaged, a damaged one was left as is for a memorial, and two were rebuilt. However, not many Germans attend church. Of those who do, 90% are Lutheran.

We spent an especially enjoyable day with Tom in Worpswede, an artists' colony. Original artworks were displayed and offered for sale. Descendants of one famous artist opened part of his house for visitors. His paintings lined the walls. Needlework and other crafts were offered for sale. Masterpieces of flower arrangements were everywhere. We lunched at a charming, mellow, old-looking restaurant surrounded by exquisite landscaping. The town is modest, its small houses glorified by marvelous flowers.

The only parts of the trip I didn't like were the long painful sitting times on the plane over and back. I ate too much from boredom, so it took a while to shed pounds I'd put on with unaccustomed food. It was a wonderful trip, nevertheless.

One of the most active years of my life was 1984. I had special times with my wider family and many weeks of travel. Thinking that not all three Elderhostel offerings in the catalog would be available, I applied for all of them; all three applications were accepted. These three were the first of fifteen Elderhostel weeks I enjoyed during subsequent years. On the way to the first one in Vermont, at the end of April, I flew first to Ohio to visit Mother and Webster, who was not well.

My next stop was Washington D.C. to see nephew Douglas Bosco. As a busy congressman, he had limited time for me, but he generously took me to dinner one evening and to a dinner meeting with a group of legislators who met regularly to discuss peace-seeking matters. Speakers included Roger Fisher and others I "knew" from media. Doug had to leave early, so he asked me to write a summary of what they had to say. I was delighted to do this.

Doug's secretary made a hotel reservation for me and smoothed arrangements for visits to C-SPAN, to the Library of Congress, and to the *Washington Post*. I toured the Capitol with Doug.

From there, I flew to Boston to meet Harold Shively. He showed me Bunker Hill College, where he was president and founder. I was impressed by the vocational facilities he had helped design. I liked even more the process for individualized programs to help students find ways to meet course requirements even after initial lack of success. They could take advantage of procedures that had interested me when I was teaching. When students had not fully met knowledge and skill objectives by the end of the semester, they negotiated ways to make up deficiencies instead of getting failing grades and having to take the whole course over, even when they had succeeded with some of the requirements. Options included use of tapes, tutoring, and make-up seminars.

I enjoyed getting acquainted with "Shive (Harold)'s" wife B.J. (Beverly), a former sociology professor at Bunker Hill, and also her daughter Keisha. I spent a few days with them in their Ipswich home and in walks around the neighborhood.

I took a bus to Brattleboro, Vermont, where the Elderhostel title was "Experiment in International Living." Courses included a history of relations between the U.S. and Russia, another in Spanish for beginners, and a course in non-violent resolution of conflict. We had meals and fascinating discussions with young students from all over the world. I flew home from there.

My guardian angel must have inspired me to accept all three of these Elderhostel weeks, for a most fortuitous coincidence brought me to Ohio again, this time at the exact moment when I could be of most help to Mother. Before arriving there, John and I had spent a June week driving through beautiful deserts, Utah red and green hills, Colorado cliffs by tree-lined rushing streams, the rolling countryside of Nebraska, boring Illinois, and finally a two-day visit with David and Joel at Boy Scout camp. Helen and Melissa were touring Europe with a music group.

In the few days before going to Bluffton, there was time to talk over the urgent situation at the Ewings' home. Webster's condition after a stroke had become quite worrisome, and he had at long last been persuaded that it might become impossible for him to stay any longer at the home he had lived in all his life. We had long talks about various possibilities. John took a plane home.

While I was in Bluffton, we kept the phones busy as we continued to think about the coming decision. In spite of the worry, I enjoyed being back on the campus where I had spent two memorable years nearly a half-century before. Many old landmarks were gone, but enough remained to help me relive those years. I renewed acquaintance with many people I had known.

I especially enjoyed one of our three Elderhostel courses, which involved visiting nearby homes to explore folk arts, such as woodworking, needlecrafts, and herbs. One man made canes from as many varieties of wood as he could collect. If anyone brought a variety he didn't already have he'd make them a cane from it. When I got home, I sent him some eucalyptus and live oak wood and he returned two canes. One had numerous samples glued together. At a college program to which the community was invited, I accompanied a man singing "Ave Maria" and I played "Arabesque" by Debussy.

A Bluffton man who had spent years as a social worker told me about a facility in Findlay, which sounded ideal for Mother and Webster. Weinbrenner's is sponsored by the Church of God, which also sponsors Findlay College. There are ten small cottages adjacent to a "self-help" building where residents have single rooms. Both groups have their noon meal with the nurses, who watch over them and are on call for emergencies. The third building is for extended care or nursing. The shifting from one facility to another can be accomplished easily when needed.

By the following week, the decision was made. I drove Mom around town on various errands and helped her pack boxes of things to give away or sell. A one-bedroom cottage was immediately available but they might be able to move into a two-bedroom place in a week or two. According to the Robin,

> In the meantime, as you can imagine, there is much trauma and confusion as Alyce and I help Mom sort out her stuff to decide what to take along, what to sell or give away, and what to put aside for later decisions. Most excess furniture, including a one-month-old refrigerator and an almost new electric stove, will be picked up by Auction Barn. Alyce's girls will have a garage sale with some of the smaller items. A few keepsakes were put aside for you-all.

> Yesterday was pans, dishes, and vases day. It is incredible the number of flower containers Mom has been given down through the years and are crowded onto two top closet shelves. Most were used only once or twice, I imagine. It makes you realize how reasonable it would be to dispose of these little goodies as you go along, when you have more time to make discriminating selections. As I handed things down, Mom called out "Save!" or "Sell!" as Alyce put them in separate boxes. I'm glad to report that Mother will have enough in the "save" category to provide for any flowers that come her way during the next two or three centuries!

The Toledo Elderhostel was held at the art museum where I had spent many hours as a child, when I had spent summer weeks with Grandma Poe within walking distance of the museum. We had lodging and meals at Toledo University. At the end of the week, I met Donna at the airport.

We had a final visit in McComb, then a day or so with David before driving home by way of Rocky Mountain National Park, where we had some enjoyable hikes. We stopped to see Wayne's brother in Salt Lake City and at Mary's and Edna's. Maybe Donna didn't enjoy the Scott Joplin and other Ragtime tapes as much as I did as we drove the two thousand miles, but they are etched in my memory so that I never again hear them without reliving this trip with my dear Donna.

As if there hadn't been enough adventures for one year, John and I spent nearly a month overseas. In September, we went to London and had a tour to Wales before "Painting in Purbeck" in Sunnydown. Of course, John did the painting while I took snapshots, renewed acquaintance with the hosts and "Bill" Bayly, the teacher, and relived the lovely place where I had been with Mary Johnston three years before.

A member of the class, Jean Gasson, had her car there, so she drove some of us around to the various sites where painters set up their easels. She also took Phyllis O'Neal, John, and me to explore and take pictures at other villages and beauty spots.

After the watercolor class, John and I spent hours in London museums, especially art museums. We were both drawn to Constable's exquisite drawings and watercolors. He had intended them only as rough drafts for paintings he would do later in oils, but I liked them better than the few finished paintings on display there. His trees are especially wonderful.

I was especially intrigued by Gainsborough's remarkable glass paintings. There were fewer than a dozen of these tucked away in an alcove adjacent to the Constable works. The artist's aim was to achieve maximum contrast between light and dark parts of the painting. While the best possible contrast achievable by ordinary paintings was said to be a twenty-to-one spread, these glass paintings had a 780-to-one contrast, about the same as nature on a sunny day. They were lit from behind by light bulbs, though Gainsborough, of course, had only candles. Our favorites were night views, one of a cottage in the moonlight, another a woodland scene with a lovely tree, stumps, sheep, and a pond.

I was intensely absorbed by displays in the Natural History Museum. Life-size displays showed the observations of natural phenomena that led Darwin to develop, step by step, his theory of evolution. How very well done and convincing! But purely factual and honest.

Two tours completed our month, one to the beautiful Lake Country, the other to Scotland. I'm sorry not to have notes about these trips, only a few photos and postcards. I do have a lingering memory of a special dinner in Scotland where I tasted flavors and textures I hadn't encountered before and haven't since.

# UPS AND DOWNS

Early the following year I wrote this in the Robin:

Dears:

I write this with a heavy heart, having just finished a letter to Mary Johnston's family. Did you all know she died of cancer? I enjoyed her company so very much when we had gone to England and Germany together. Our delayed friendship was precious to me; for some reason we had not been so close in high school. We stayed in contact after the trip and had planned to travel together again. Her son Tom is such a special young man, working for peace in the State Department.

Have you noticed how quickly time goes by these days? There are certain things I always do on Fridays. Now when Friday comes around, I am always surprised: "It can't be Friday already." I am reminded of the clock David put together when he was a little kid. I had bought him a kit for a wooden wall clock. He had to figure out all the gears and mechanisms, following written directions. He was quite good at anything requiring manual skill and a sense of spatial relationships, but being somewhat behind in reading, it was a fine project for him. He worked on it for days, as I remember, and finally called us all to come see him set it off. He wound it up and let go. The big hand went around about twenty times as fast as an ordinary second hand and the hours went zap, zap,

zap … We all had a hearty laugh. But now the laugh is on me, for that's the way my life is going!

Juliet is still absorbed with horses, to the point that she plans now to make horsemanship her life work one way or another. She has her own horse, which she rides, feeds, and grooms every day. Usually Judy drives her to the stables and Myrl picks her up on his way home from work. But he is down below La Paz on an oceanographic project this month. I suppose Juliet will be driving in another year.

The last week of the year her family, Tim, a girlfriend, John, and I spent a few days at the Mehling Ranch in Baja California. Judy's family goes there often. This beautiful place in unspoiled countryside has horses to ride; it's not too expensive. Thirty some guests have delicious meals around one long table. We played games around the fireplace in a house our extended family had all to itself, rugged, kerosene lamps, no meals to cook.

One day on a ride my horse was balky and wouldn't go. Juliet said she'd fix it. She got on, took a few trots, and gave it back to me. No more problems. I have no idea what she did.

Karl is majoring in music at UCSD, not the kind any of you would like. He's a sweet young man. He lives in a house with four other male students. He had us all for Christmas Eve. He served us nibbles and eggnog and made each family a big decorated jar of mulled cider with a computer-written message and "directions for use" pasted on the outside. It is delightful to get results of the kids' efforts rather than something that costs money. Gail has also left home. She's in an apartment with friends and has a steady job with a boyfriend's father who puts custom things in cars.

My first grandchild Karl has an interesting history. When he was born with a twisted "club foot," he was fitted with a plaster cast until he was old enough to walk. We were amused by the "danger" of getting whammed by his leg as he was lifted from the crib. His first shoes continued the reshaping process; the problem disappeared.

Years later, on the first day of summer vacation, he went to try out his new skateboard in the place that had been built for skateboard use, probably to prevent kids' skating on the sidewalks. The speed and force of going down that bowl-like place forced his leg up through his pelvis and fractured it. I remember playing games with him as he lay in a hospital bed, his leg in traction. The doctor predicted it would be a year before he could walk, but he was OK when school started in the fall.

By this time, his family was living near Valhalla High School. When the Gruenewalds had lived about seven years in the Anza house, they too found two acres more land than they wanted to take care of. Its value had increased sixfold, and it was even more ripe for development. It sold quickly, to the financial benefit of both families. After a good down payment, the buyer stalled on the balance, became bankrupt, and left the owner of the second trust to pay the rest. The new owner rented the house for a while, then built condos, as I had planned.

In the eighties, I participated in six more Elderhostels, many of them with John. Edna and Carl Lingenfelter joined us in one in Idyllwild. When all four of us checked in together with Edna in crutches after a broken leg, they gave us excellent rooms in a small house. We had two large master bedrooms with baths separated by a living room with a fireplace. There was a porch overlooking the campus. We explored surrounding woods, enjoyed Vivaldi music, and played bridge after hours.

Late in the week, I developed a strange, persistent pain across my middle. Though my sister was an RN, she was equally baffled. She and Carl had driven down from Novato because they were coming home with us at the end of the week. This made it possible for me to leave John with them, take our car a day early, and head for a doctor. As I left quite early in the morning, there was little traffic, so I drove too fast and got a ticket. It turned out that I had shingles. Diagnosing it quickly and treating it with topical ointment and pills helped.

Another Elderhostel was in Cedar City, Utah. A geology professor fascinated me with his descriptions and a film showing the history of our continent. I loved two outdoor Shakespeare plays with preliminary antics making it all feel authentic. Another course took advantage of the area's rich variety of wildflowers, which we were thrilled to discover on daily hikes.

Two women joined me at the Keystone Science School in Colorado. The main attraction there was cross-country skiing. We slept in bunk beds in log cabins a short walk from the dining and program room. Alas, on the first morning, on the way to breakfast, I stepped on snow that covered slippery ice and fell, giving my head a hard thump. It took help from a clinic and two days of recovery before I was fitted with skis and joined the others on an uphill effort. The top of the hill was worth the effort of getting there, but going back down was another story.

John and I went together to Nogales, Arizona. Driving south from Tucson a bit early, we noticed some building going on along the highway, with advertising signs about Green Valley, so we decided to have a look. New dwellings were attractive and just the right size, the day was so pleasantly warm, the sky was so blue and so beautifully decorated with white fluffy clouds that we began to wonder whether this might be a better place to live than where we were. The more we investigated the community the more seductive it became. The vastness of the sunny sky and the powerful mountain view had us seriously considering buying a condo and moving there—until we came to our senses as we got advance symptoms of homesickness.

We had courses in indigenous arts and culture, on cattle ranches in the area, and another dealing with relations between the U.S. and Mexico. We spent free time enjoying the many beauties of nature nearby. One day, we shopped and dined across the border in Mexico.

We thoroughly enjoyed the Elderhostel in Taos, New Mexico. I took dozens of pictures near and around the historic Mabel Dodge Luhan house where we stayed. Its twenty-two rooms are filled with art and artifacts of the Southwest. We heard stories of famous and interesting people who had been there. We enjoyed a great mountain view and trips to admire original paintings in local shops. One unique feature here: we took turns cleaning vegetables, cooking, and cleaning up in the kitchen. A great way to get acquainted and learn new recipes!

Most Elderhostel directions provide practical ways of getting there. Until information arrived about the course at Bloomsburg, Pennsylvania, in which I had enrolled, I had no idea how necessary it would be to have a car. So this was my first experience of renting one. Maps took me safely out of Philadelphia and to a dorm room at the university. Two courses were the most absorbing. Mozart was a favorite composer of mine, and I had not only seen the play *Amadeus* in England, but had also read a book about this famous story. I came to Bloomsburg with much concern about the safety of nuclear energy. The professor and a trip to the nuclear facilities captured my attention and somewhat relieved my anxieties.

On the drive back to Philadelphia, I was surprised by living conditions in an area of mining country I had never seen. I went to Hershey for two days where they are well equipped to show us tourists how they produce chocolate—and ready to sell us some before we go. Of course, I bought some. Soon after this trip, I was visiting David's family just after Joel had graduated from high school. I was prepared.

We give our grandchildren a gift worth about $1,000 when they graduate. At the supper table I gave Joel a card of congratulation attached to a bag of chocolate kisses and a box of chocolates to pass around. I said, "This is not your real gift, Joel." He piped up, "It must be stock in the Hershey Company." It was! I figured that he was already OK for college expenses. Kids his age waste money, but a dividend now and then would be pleasant and then he could sell the stock at greater value later when he really needed it. I think he used it years later toward a down payment for a house.

Through the eighties Robin letters kept making the rounds. Here is a sample of the way we included silly jokes and slices of the more trivial aspects of our aging lives along with our griefs.

Dear Mother, et al,

I start with you, Mom, because I spent the last three hours suffering and seeking that letter of Mary's that I promised to send you. I had put it in the safest place possible–I thought. But when I went to get it, it wasn't there. But it had to be! Then followed searches in about twenty other places I might have put it instead. I looked in every folder, every file drawer, pile of clippings, book, or magazine that I had had anything to do with in the previous week. I looked in the League of Women Voters stuff, the Great Decisions stuff, paper by paper. I looked on the bulletin board, a folder in the car of things to photocopy, in my other purse, under the sofa. Then I started over. Some of these places were subjected to three or four close examinations. In the drawer where it was supposed to be, I looked about five times. But no.

My blood pressure must have gone way up for my face was feeling flushed. My tummy was burning, so I stopped and ate an apple and read something and listened to the weather report on TV (We had 2 ½ inches of rain today.) At last, I decided to look once more in the bill drawer where it was supposed to be before throwing myself on the mercy of the court. I took everything out, piece by piece. Eureka! There it was! And now I know why I had not recognized it earlier. Back at Mother's, this letter had been the only thing lying on the desk when I had phoned Greyhound, so I had penciled the schedule on the back of it. In previous searches, I hadn't looked at *both* sides of every paper.

Not all of you heard on the phone about my fall from the apple tree. No, you jokers, not "trying to be a branch manager" (Alyce), not "learning the Apple computer" (Mary), not "testing the sap" (Edna). The sap was pretending to be twelve again by going after some hard-to-reach beauties. It was working, too, until a branch broke and down came Carol, apple and all.

I write this on my new toy, a word processor. My old typewriter was driving me crazy. It would shiver and complain when I tried to return to the left-hand margin and then it wouldn't go all the way. It would misspell words and then when I tried to correct them, using those little bits of white paper they make for the purpose, I couldn't get them in the right space because the typewriter had variable spacing and I couldn't always remember whether a letter took one, two, or three spaces. (Alas, again, for memory.) When I shopped for a new typewriter, I found that this outfit didn't cost much more than the IBM I had planned to get. It's taking a while to get the hang of it, but having worked with a similar one at the university, I'm finally understanding the little beauty.

A recent pleasure was Mary's visit. When she left, I missed the sound of her voice and the "something special about today" feeling I had when I wakened in the morning and remembered she was still here, asleep in the study.

Writing these next lines was exceedingly difficult. My heart still aches when I remember how hard it was for Mother throughout her dying days. She didn't deserve a painful death! I can't forget how helpless I felt as I tried to ease things for her.

I first heard of her trouble when John and I were renting a Green Valley apartment for a week. Alyce's husband Gene called to say that Mother was in the hospital with a serious heart attack. I couldn't get an immediate flight from Tucson, so I decided to go home and try San

Diego airlines. Then Edna, our family RN, went to her, and I wasn't needed just then to help Alyce and Gene take care of her. After a while, Edna went home and I went.

Though Mother's pain was helped somewhat by regular injections, extreme discomfort seemed the worst part. She was hungry but couldn't swallow, thirsty but couldn't drink. She was miserable all over and couldn't sleep. She repeatedly said she wanted to die. I never saw the doctor, but I phoned him pleading for stronger medicine. He said he wasn't "into euthanasia."

At night, I slept in her cottage a few feet across the alley from the caring facility. Nurses left a back door open to go out and smoke, and they didn't object to my coming in to check on her on and off through the night. She welcomed my visit. If she needed something, it didn't help to press a button: a night nurse might not know that she couldn't hear, so she'd ask, "What is it Mrs. Ewing?" but not follow up if there was no answer. One night, I found her suffering so much pain that I went to the nurses' station. I was told that they had skipped her regular injection because she had been asleep when they came by.

Some of the family were with her shortly before she died. They left for lunch and she was gone when they returned. When I finally could bear to do it, I wrote this:

*October 25, 1988*
Dear Girls,

I have been reluctant to do my bit in the Robin this time. I think it's because I always sent it to Mother before, so whenever I began to consider what I'd write about, the pain of losing her would return in full force. It was like pulling the scab off a wound that was trying to heal, but was mighty slow doing it. I keep reliving the agony of that last week with her and my anger at what I considered unsatisfactory treatment.

Now came a momentous day and a superlative celebration, our Golden Wedding Day! We felt that one day wasn't enough. And we wanted to mark our fifty-year achievement in a way that fit our rather unconventional family. We followed custom when we had a portrait made by a professional photographer and sent it to the newspaper with an announcement, but when the kids asked how we wanted to celebrate, we told them what we *didn't* want: the usual dress-up reception that our friends would feel obligated to attend and bring presents even if invitations said "no gifts please."

So Judy suggested a family camping trip in memory of some of our best family times. We wouldn't have to go far: Lake Jennings campground is just across the lake. She reserved a long weekend for four campsites, including our favorite one close to the lake. John and I used the "turtle" (our mini-camper). Other sites were used by Donna and Wayne, here from Utah, and David, from Indiana by plane. Still others were occupied by local family members, including grandchildren and assorted spouses. Tim came after work every day.

By the special day, April 16, 1989, our dear family and a few friends were here with us. John's brother George sent an enormous basket of flowers, which served as centerpiece on the picnic table. Over it was a screened ramada, which Judy had bought and decorated with a colorful garland. For breakfast, Gail brought four kinds of fresh bagels and cream cheese. For the banquet, Judy and Donna produced five vegetarian salads: potato, tabbouleh, pasta, ratatouille, and three-bean. Tim brought barbecued chicken and a two-tiered cake, which John and I were obliged to cut—and do the bride-feeds-groom bit after champagne toasts and a walk under arched arms to the tune of the wedding march. Later they even threw rice! They gave us gifts too, despite our don'ts.

We filled our plates and sat on rocks under the trees, looking out over the lake and listening to serenading mocking birds. Cameras clicked throughout the weekend. Some people went boating; some played the new game I got for my birthday, "Pictionary." Everyone hiked—a few went six miles around the lake—and some mostly just "hung out." We finished the weekend by driving to our house across from the lake and reminiscing.

Sadly, John's brother Phil was not with us. He died the month before of fibrosis of the lungs. Like John, he had stopped smoking, but not soon enough. His death was not unexpected, for when he suffered an acute episode a few months before, he was told he had only a few months to live. When his time came, it wasn't as bad as Mother's ordeal. He was using oxygen and not feeling too bad until a day or so before the end. John had even taken him out for lunch when he was staying with Kaye after his first hospital trip.

Not all of my travels during the eighties were Elderhostel trips. Two others were memorable; in each there was a forecast of troubles to come in the nineties. The first one started as a sudden impulse of mine. David's family was sitting around the picnic table on our patio, talking of their flight plans for returning home. "Melissa," I said, "how about staying here another day or two and I'll drive you home?" We had recently bought a slightly used Volvo, safe and fun to drive. It would be nice to have this delightful granddaughter along to help drive and help enjoy the Grand Canyon and other special places along the way. John was a bit tired of travel. The idea caught hold immediately. Yes! She'd like that!

For one of Melissa's fine pictures of the Grand Canyon, she wanted one of the sun coming up over a mountain. We set the alarm clock and took some perfect photos. Riding the old train from Durango, Colorado, to Silverton was a highlight of the trip. We were amazed that the tracks had been laid on such a narrow strip of land. A rushing river at the right seemed dangerously close; if windows had been open, we could have touched the cliffs at the left.

In planning our route, I had selected destinations for motel reservations, but I hadn't allowed enough time to reach Santa Fe until very late. Weary and not quite awake, as Melissa took the key toward the motel room, I opened the trunk to get the suitcases. She came back and said, "Oh, Grandma, this is the wrong room number."

Exasperated, I slammed the trunk door shut. Car keys were resting inside on one of the suitcases! It took many phone calls to solve the problem this late at night. The few helpful people I was able to reach referred me to someone else. Nothing worked for at least an hour, while Melissa kept feeding me change for the phone. Meanwhile, she made her daily call home on another phone. When I finally reached a locksmith, he still had a Volkswagen yet to do and he hadn't had a bite to eat yet, but promised he'd be there in an hour or two.

Relieved but bone weary I turned to Melissa to report the good news. But she had news too, "Grandpa had a stroke today and he's in the hospital." Waiting in the motel room, I had no fear of falling asleep: I was thinking about the quickest way to get home. When Melissa fell asleep, I turned the room light off and went to the bathroom and tried to read. Naturally, that was impossible, but I figured out a plan.

Since both Melissa and I drive, we'd take turns driving and sleeping and go straight to Indiana, stopping only for gas and phone. David would make me a plane reservation the next day and I'd leave the car there. All went according to plan. As soon as I got home, John was ready to leave the hospital. In a couple of months, he was driving and playing golf. Helen's brother drove the Volvo home.

John's second trip to London with me started quite smoothly. We had learned better ways of getting there. My friend Jane was a travel agent; she got us tickets through the polar route, which was shorter. Also, she made sure we did not arrive in the morning as we had done before and had to wait around half asleep in the lobby before we had access to our room. She got us seats at the bulkhead where we'd have leg room and could more easily get up and walk in the aisle.

After a 2:30 arrival at Gatwick, an efficient check-in process, the train to Victoria Station, and a cab to Vandon House, we still had time to drop our bags and walk back to Victoria in order to buy tickets for plays and tours. While I waited in line for almost an hour, John strolled around the station, checking by from time to time. Then an unbelievable coincidence: the man behind me in line heard me spell my name to the ticket agent. He asked if by any chance I happened to know a David Straubinger from Indiana! "Why, yes! He's my son!" This man, Charles Rader, a bassoon player, knew him from the Indianapolis Symphony Orchestra, knew all about David's family, his business, and his woodwind quintet. After he got his tickets, he took John and me to meet his fellow travelers, who also knew David well. What are the odds of this happening?

Before leaving home, I wrote to Jean Gasson, who had driven us around to various painting sites when we were together at Sunnydown in 1985. She phoned us the first evening, inviting us to her home in Bournemouth for a day's drive to familiar spots. Next morning she met us at the train station with a surprise, Phyllis O'Neill, the third painter in the 1985 foursome.

We all had lunch at Jean's and admired her remodeled house and garden, then rode to the stone cottage at Sunnydown on the coast, not far from Bournemouth. We chatted a few minutes with host Julie and then had "cream tea" in a familiar nearby village. Or was it a hamlet? Probably not a town, though it did have a church. These definitions are specific in England. A city must have a cathedral. Size doesn't distinguish a city from a town.

We rode a train back to London with Phyllis and made plans to take a cruise up the Thames to see Kew Gardens the Sunday before we were to leave. That cruise didn't happen. The week before, a tragic accident had stopped all traffic on the river. A tugboat had collided with a pleasure boat having a night party. Many were drowned.

Newscasts were full of details. One interview with a survivor stands out in my memory. Being on the upper deck, he had a better chance. Swept overboard, he tried to come to the surface and swim to shore, but he came up under one of the vessels. Imagine not knowing which direction to swim to get clear! Many didn't. And the ones on the lower deck had no chance at all.

Our tour to Paris took all day—a long bus ride to Dover, the Hovercraft across the channel, and another bus ride to Paris where we met an agent of Frames Tours. He gave us hotel vouchers, and tickets for two tours, one on a Seine boat, and another for a special bus that circled the main tourist spots. Our hotel was exceptionally pleasant; the breakfasts were wonderful. One could choose from a wide variety of fresh fruits, croissants, cheeses, yogurts, eggs, sausages, bacon, and superb coffee, and the service was excellent.

Alas, we had a most worrying problem. When we had dinner the first night with a delightful couple, John was not his usual self and his appetite was poor. The next morning, when we returned to our room after breakfast, he was feeling so miserable that he worried about angina and took a nitroglycerin pill. This proved disastrous. He groaned and went limp, then began to shake as if he was about to have convulsions. I phoned the desk and they immediately sent up an English-speaking doctor.

John's blood pressure was very low because the nitro had enhanced the effect of dehydration. He had had almost no water the day before as we were herded from bus to boat to bus. He had even taken his Norpace without water. The doctor gave him an injection and me a prescription to fill for his stomach. He improved miraculously but stayed in the room until late in the afternoon. For lunch, we ordered from an excellent, reasonably priced room service menu.

Then I set out on the bus tour. I didn't enjoy lurching around angled streets to get quick glimpses of the city, so when the driver announced that we would stop for a while at the Eiffel tower, I decided to get off and walk back to the hotel. I wrote this account about what happened next:

> I seemed to remember that the Tuileries were across the river and to the left a few blocks. After taking photos of the Chaillot Palace, the gardens, and fountains, I walked up to the street and walked and walked and walked, trying to decipher how my map connected with the street signs.
>
> Wherever I turned, I became more baffled. About the time my feet were threatening to give up completely, some kind folks whose pointing was more comprehensible than their language came to my rescue. I got a bus to the hotel. My main problem was not knowing north from south. What a help a good magnet would have been. Actually, the Tuileries were to the right of the palace, not the left. Was the map upside down—south on top? Is that possible?

On our evening walk, we came upon a carnival full of exuberant people, games, rides, booths, and a towering slide that led riders swiftly down to bouncy landings and screams of delight. We had ice cream cones and a feeling of being invisible ghosts on another planet.

Plans for the next days were out of phase with our energies but we did enjoy the essential Paris experience, a long time having something refreshing in an outdoor café as we watched people go by. John's tummy was clearly OK by now, for he had a huge banana split. I had a heavenly orange ice in a frozen orange cup.

Walks took us back to the gardens, along tempting garments in a Laura Ashley shop and in a Cardin window. We took a bus to see some ugly Picasso originals in a new museum with smelly toilets and no paper. Back across the river, we took pictures from the top of the Eiffel tower. We weren't in Paris the right day for a tour to the Monet gardens.

Back in London, we saw four plays for which we already had tickets. First was the famous musical *Cats*, which we found disappointing. Costumes and special effects were spectacular and we enjoyed the dancing. We were fortunate to have tickets in a full house with dozens waiting hopefully outside, but the music was so loud we had to hold our hands over our ears half the time. Both this and the musical *M. Butterfly* were matinees.

Peter Shaffer's *Lettice and Lovage* was the third play. We were greatly amused by this comedy. In the opening scene, Lettice stood at the foot of a curving staircase in a historical house giving her spiel to successive groups of visitors. Starting with a typical recitation of prosaic facts about former owners, dates, etc., she began to make a few changes for each succeeding group, each change adding more drama to the story of a significant fall down those stairs. By and by, informed listeners challenged her "facts," which were given gamely and defended in her most haughty and authoritarian manner until a National Trust director joined a group to follow up on some shocking reports she had been hearing about Lettice's inventive tales. "But the facts were so boring and people enjoyed my stories and left such nice tips" failed to justify the changes to the straight-laced supervisor.

Until we saw *Les Miserables*, I couldn't imagine it as a musical, but it worked. Staging, acting, music were superb. My appreciation was enhanced by having taken a copy of Victor Hugo's book along on the trip and reading about a third of it in advance. This play was my favorite. The Shaffer was fun, but this one was astounding—a huge undertaking. No wonder it was the most expensive and popular. It's a good thing we got tickets before leaving home.

We spent less time in museums than in 1984. We revisited Victoria and Albert. I especially wanted to have another look at Gainsborough's glass paintings. Obviously one can only sample the rooms of this art museum. One room had various paintings depicting literary characters. On the way to the Constable section, we passed by a temporary showing of nudes. Back on the first floor, I spent all the time I wanted at the extensive exhibit of historical fashions I had discovered in 1985 just a few minutes before closing time. I was eager to revisit the Natural History Museum with John. He was as impressed as I had been by displays showing the evolution of species.

*April 30, 1989*
For the benefit of Irene way over in Israel, here are a few happenings. Early in the month, John and I drove up to see the folks

in the north. On the way up, we stayed overnight with Karl and Jeannie in their compact L.A. apartment. It's amazing to see how smoothly they have arranged their sound equipment, two computers, books, piano, etc. Jeannie is going to college full time, studying communications. Her enthusiasm is contagious. Karl is doing "music engraving" using a MacIntosh program to transfer rough-draft music notation to printable form. These two still enjoy producing creative music, but it isn't paying the bills.

The first morning after we arrived at Edna's in Novato and enjoyed her excellent cuisine, John felt quite dizzy but needed to go to the bathroom, so I helped him get up. He took one step out of bed and collapsed on the floor. We wakened Edna and Carl. They called paramedics, who phoned ahead for details and had him in intensive care at Kaiser in short order. Surprisingly, it was not another stroke, as I had feared, but pneumonia. He had been feeling cold: weighing only 111 pounds, he had no padding.

When we saw him at the hospital the next morning he felt fine, despite oxygen tubing in his nose and intravenous fluids coming in his arm. However, he was kept in the hospital almost a week. We kept in touch by phone and frequent visits—only six miles from Edna's. I drove north to Sebastopol to see Mary in her "new" mobile home with its "new" piano.

I had a wonderful visit with my namesake Caroll about her work with the prisoner work crew. She's a truly fine woman. I had supper with Doug and Gayle in their superb new home.

### August 3, 1990

John had his throat stretched again. It's a trying experience for him, but it helps to keep the passageway open. Otherwise he has real problems getting the food to go down. I worry about him. He keeps losing weight, now 109 pounds!

Tomorrow Michael and his three kids and wife are coming for lunch. Mike will have a look at a project he'll do for us: replacing our little pool with a patio.

The pool was lovely, but John just can't keep up with the need for periodic cleaning. Besides, it leaks and we are having a severe water shortage.

*(A few years later, a fox mother squeezed into a space below the new patio and gave birth to five babies. She brought the little balls of furry charm out for a frolic about suppertime every night. We and neighbors watched with delight from our picture windows as they took their first steps and grew rapidly into frolicking adolescents. They climbed the trees as their mama watched from her perch on a tall rock. One evening the father paid a visit.)*

Tomorrow evening we go to the airport to get Mary for a few days' visit ... One more news flash: I'm going to be a *great grand-mother*! Gail will be the mommy.

### November 11, 1990

Judy left last weekend for a month in India, her third trip there. There's a sort of retreat where she and some close friends go. Their leader is a spiritual teacher named Si Baba. Judy and Juliet are now on a completely vegetarian diet.

### April 8, 1991

Gail's baby came: eight-pound Jessica. Monday as John golfed, mother and baby spent a half day with me. What a joy to cuddle a soft, sleepy, contented newborn. I'm seeing more of Tara these days. What a live wire! She loves to be chased, to laugh with delight, to dance, to play Tim's harmonica, to make unmistakably clear non-verbal requests for what she wants. My only regret is that she has such a short attention span that she won't sit still to be read to. She insists on turning the pages herself, roughly. You may remember her granny was (is) a book nut.

March was a month of visitors. Donna and Wayne came for a week to help with the newborn. Alyce and Gene drove over from Phoenix, where they often spend a few winter months.

It was also a month when John lost his balance standing on one leg as he put on his pajamas. I was already in bed. I heard a piercing scream followed by terrible groans of pain. I thought he was having a heart attack, but he "merely" fractured one or more ribs. It took more than three weeks before he could play golf. He also went through the colon tests requiring him to fast for two days, causing him to lose still more weight. He's down around 107 now! The doctor says he looks like a survivor of a concentration camp. Must be my cooking ... He and I are like Jack Spratt and his wife: he needs fattening food, I need the opposite.

No family event could be more tragic than the death of Caroll Bosco, so beloved by her husband, three young children, and countless others. Sad forebodings began shortly after I had enjoyed the visit with her mentioned in the April '89 letter above. She had breast cancer. Every effort was made to save her life. Doug had forgone his reelection campaign to concentrate on helping his beloved sister. When Mary flew down for a short visit with me in April '91, we were torn between despairing of Caroll's worsening condition and grasping at hope of a miracle. But the ensuing months brought only more pain and finally resignation.

A few weeks after Mary's visit she called to say that if I wanted to see Caroll once more, I had better come up soon. I did. I cherish the memory of those few moments I spent with my dear namesake, saying the unsayable good-bye by holding her hand and reading her favorite Bible selections to her. Mary was still being torn apart by feeling one moment, "It just cannot, will not happen", and the next moment, "I'm afraid it will and I can't bear it!" I know that it is unrealistic to think I could feel her pain as intensely as she did, but I like to think I shared enough of her burden to help a little. In a few months, I wrote the following in the Robin:

> The memorial service was beautiful. Chairs were set up in Doug's parking lot, facing his redwood forest with rhododen-dron flowers peeking through. Caroll's musical friends played her favorite songs and hymns. Her closest friends—and especially Doug—movingly told what her life had meant to them and to the many others who knew and loved her ...
>
> There followed much visiting among those who hadn't seen each other for quite a while. They could view photos of Caroll doing happy things with family and friends. There was a delicious buffet for hundreds served on Doug's spacious patio. We found comfort in hugging each other and watching the antics of Doug and Gayle's baby boy Johnny.
>
> Judy and David were both there. Judy had developed a special

relationship with Mary and Caroll when she lived in San Francisco ... David combined this family affair with a needed business trip to Oakland ...

Someone said there were 150 cars parked along Doug's roadways; there were two shuttle buses. In one bus were some of the offenders Caroll had supervised. Caroll had told me about the prisoners' regard for her. A new man on the work crew would be quickly set straight by the others if he was not respectful to her. Once when she complimented one fellow by saying, "Good job, Joe!" he had shed tears and said, "That's the first time anyone ever said that to me."

Even though "Down" events were the most important through the nineties, they were interspersed with travels and good times at Elderhostels and family reunions. Actually, the reunions started in 1986 when John's older brother George, living nearby at the time, suggested the plan that became a series of six Straubinger family reunions held in alternate years in a variety of states. One day when Phil was with them, the three brothers had been reminiscing about growing up in Kansas with their three cousins, Matilda, Dorothy, and Katherine, now married with families.

The cousins and their husbands were invited to come to San Diego for a week of vacation and family get-togethers. George reserved adjacent rooms in a Mission Valley hotel as well as a large banquet room. All three couples came. According to happy faces in my folder of snapshots, they really enjoyed themselves.

A photo of the three sisters in front of the three brothers taken on our patio is especially delightful. An artist friend of mine came and drew caricatures of everyone. At the banquet and at a picnic at Donna's by the swimming pool, the Kansans became acquainted with our California families. Between times, they used rental cars to enjoy the famous attractions of the area.

Two years later, similar family groups met in Kansas. This time we met *their* children and grandchildren. Supper at Tillie's and brunch next morning at Dorothy's were followed by dinner at the hotel with speeches, more pictures, and chatting around the hotel pool. There were dozens of stories to share in hours and hours of conversation there and in our rooms. Younger brother Don and his wife joined us this time. He was doing quite well after a recent heart transplant.

He invited us to come to Tallahassee, Florida, next time with as many of our extended families as could come. He had so many hospitable children living close by that we didn't need a hotel. We had our main dinner in his beach house. Young ones enjoyed swimming in the ocean, jumping on a trampoline, and riding on a river boat through jungle habitat with alligators and other creatures. One Florida family has children named Adam and Erin Straubinger. Phil's son and wife had named two of theirs Adam and Erin Straubinger!

Donna did the planning, letters, and reservations in Salt Lake City for the fourth reunion in 1992. Judy went early and helped with the shopping and cooking for the usual Friday night supper in Bountiful, the suburb where the Gruenewalds lived. I was so proud of my daughters, impressed by their delicious food and by how well they worked together. We enjoyed their production on the patio, surrounded by greenery and flowers. Stepping-stones led up a slope to a space with a hot tub and view.

Donna had reserved the hotel's "penthouse" apartment for John and me. It had a bedroom, kitchen, dining room, and, in the living room, a large U-shaped sofa looking toward the city. Relatives brought their continental breakfasts up to join us around the table and talk, talk, talk. They spent much time in the penthouse and on the three balconies between other activities. Everyone brought a baby picture of himself or herself and we had a contest to see who could identify the most. Christopher Fair (Phil's stepson) did magic tricks and made funny animal balloons.

The Sunday picnic was held in a wonderful theme park where we wandered through extensive landscaping with sections named for several countries and designed accordingly. We also spent some time exploring fine gardens around the tabernacle. I did a little research in the Mormons' world-famous genealogy library, where I probed for information about my forbears. But it was difficult and I soon lost interest.

My son David and his children Melissa and Joel came, also Donna's children Karl and Gail. Gail's baby Jessica was barely a year old. She was a charmer, full of energy and curiosity. These reunions highlight the workings of the life cycle: by now (2008), John and his two brothers have left us, as well as George's three sons.

I spent two Elderhostel weeks during this time. I picked up Mary in Santa Rosa and drove north to Shenoa in the middle of a forest. Unique programs included earth-centered subjects like conservation and vegetarian cooking. I especially enjoyed the day when a young boy who lived there gave me a guided tour through the extensive, well kept vegetable garden which supplied our meals.

With my friend Ruth, I enjoyed Shakespeare's plays at an Elderhostel in Ashland, Oregon. Ruth's brother had recently bought a house there. We located it and visited with the present occupants. Then we spent a day being amazed by a retirement community with all levels of care for older people, even independent houses. Able dwellers had their names on specific garden plots filled with a wide variety of thriving vegetables and flowers. For years I continued getting advertising brochures tempting me to come there.

# JOHN'S STRUGGLES

Throughout our California years, John endured numerous accidents, ailments, the frightening episodes in Paris, and his first stroke. But what happened in late 1992, and on the four following years were even worse ordeals.

His first stroke had found him alone while I was half way across the country with Melissa. With great difficulty, it had taken him a while before he was able to crawl to the phone and dial 911. Recovery didn't take very long. The next time, thankfully, I was with him. There was probably no way a doctor could have predicted an imminent stroke two days before when John had been feeling so bad that we had taken him for a checkup. Edna and Carl, here on the way to an Elderhostel in Arizona, had helped me take him to the doctor before they left.

When I came into the bedroom where he sat watching TV, I found him incoherent. I was sure it was a stroke. Paramedics came, confirmed it, and took him to Kaiser. After the hospital, he went to a rehabilitation facility. Day after day, week after week, I watched him work with speech, physical, and occupational therapists. They helped him to eventually regain ability to swallow, talk (slurred and slowly), bathe (with help), shave, dress (though his right hand never recovered), and walk with a cane.

How I admired his infinite patience! And I was awed by the skill of those who knew ways to help him recover and encourage him along the way. Little by little, to lessen the pain of seeing him helpless, I had the pleasure of seeing bits of progress when I accompanied him daily to his therapy sessions. After many weeks of progress, it was a joy to have lunch with him in the dining room.

In the middle of February, he came home. Various home health care providers came day after day for two months of therapy. We continued following their directions for painstaking routines. I gave him soft foods and thickened liquids to enable swallowing; we practiced conversation as he talked slowly and took frequent breaths; he took daily walks; we played the card games he could handle.

With gradual improvement, he became able to use a cane to go all around the block. In March, he had the first of many falls. At Jessica's birthday party in a park, we all walked a couple of blocks to a playground to watch Tim's daughters and Jessica swing and slide. John sat on a bench chatting with Judy when he suddenly said he wanted to leave. On Judy's arm he shuffled over to a water fountain for a few sips and splashes to his forehead. Starting back, his knees gave out. He slumped to the grass and lay down. Nearby, young people called 911 before we knew they were doing it. They came, but it wasn't really necessary. We got him safely into the car and home.

Despite this minor setback, he kept on improving. He could even spend an Elderhostel week—right here in San Diego! We could easily pretend we had gone away, for the week was full of new experiences. Our room was in the same hotel where we had courses in sea life: bottlenose whales, dolphins, etc., along with field trips. In free time, we spent time in parts of Balboa Park we had barely noticed or been aware of before. We loved the rose garden. We looked up three different places where John had lived with Phil and his mother while he was in high school.

In July, he had a hernia operation. No problem. But a month later he simply got up from his chair and fell. I ran across the street to get help. Audrey, a retired RN, suspected a broken hip and vetoed getting him up, so we called paramedics again. Audrey was right: his hip was broken. There followed a long agonizing period of surgery followed by therapy at the Stanford rehab hospital and at home.

He was never again able to walk without a walker. He had been able to get along with a cane, but a walker requires two hands. His right hand was still useless: the fingers were turned under so that the hand is a permanent fist. I took that problem to a physician's supply store.

They helped fashion a platform on the right side of the walker on which his arm, firmly attached with a Velcro lined strap, could lift it. From this same company, we bought an electric recliner that could lift him forward so he could get out of the chair and into the walker.

Because the bad leg was now shorter, we had to have two inches added to his shoe soles. Later in the year, he fell again, on the bedroom floor. Another neighbor came and lifted him.

Nevertheless, we managed another Elderhostel, this time in Ventura. A course about the Channel Islands had drawn Carl's interest. He and Edna persuaded us to join them. They would help us get around and we would have a good time together. Our room was right across from the elevator, fortunately, for by that time John was using a walker. Classrooms were in the same hotel. A trip to the Channel Islands was canceled because of the weather but we enjoyed the ocean from a long pier and had good courses dealing with music and current events. To my surprise, traffic through L.A. happened to be unusually light both going and returning.

In '95, John walked regularly along the level part of the street in front of our house. He often encountered our neighbor Dale Simmons four doors away. She too was in a walker, recovering from surgery for a brain tumor. The two joked about a walker race. As time went on, she became a good friend and then, happily, my daughter-in-law!

One day when I returned from the grocery store, several neighbors met me with a shocking surprise. They said things like "Don't worry," and "It wasn't too bad; he'll be OK." John had been taken to the emergency room after a man backed out of his driveway and hit the walker, causing him to fall against a brick edging. Stitches closed a big gash on top of his head this time. That didn't work after one bad fall later on.

A few weeks later, he fell in the house. No one was around to help but with time I was able to get him first onto a footstool and then up to a chair.

But now came two worse falls. On the first day of December '96, I drove him to Kaiser to see his doctor about a troublesome urinary problem. He wanted to see about his prostate. After helping him out of the car and onto the sidewalk, well away from the curb (I thought), I turned back to the car to move it away from the no-parking zone. Almost immediately he tripped, whacked his head against the curb, and scraped his "best" leg on the cement sidewalk.

A flurry of white-coated helpers appeared at once, including our personal doctor who spoke of taking him to the emergency room at the hospital. I was incredulous at the thought of doing that. I was aghast at my vision of driving him seven miles or so in the shape he was in. The incident left me too nervous to be a safe driver. "Or," said the doctor, "call 911." What?! Where?!

Naturally, they all came to their senses, and by the time I parked the car, John and the white-coated folks had disappeared. I went to the doctor's quarters and found the nurse sopping blood from his head as he groaned about the pain in his right hip, the "good" one after he broke the other, though it was affected by the stroke. It took twenty hours and a pile of gauze pads before the bleeding slowed to a few drops. There was no gash to sew up; instead, a wide area of skin was scraped away. It was difficult to maintain enough pressure on the wound to stem the heavy flow of blood. The next morning, his pillow was heavy with blood. Healing was slow.

Tim widened our back stairs to fit the walker, but three months after the last episode, John came back from a walk and missed the bottom step. Hearing a sound of dismay, I rushed out to find him flat on his back on the carport with blood rushing from his head again! Petey next door caught Ab across the street just as he was about to leave.

As Jim Abercrombie had been a navy corpsman, he rescued us with great skill. He wrapped three old towels tightly around John's head to put pressure on the wound and then helped him get into the car. Five hours and several stitches later, we got back home to wash the blood out of our clothes. Our dear neighbor had even washed the blood off our carport before going on his way!

One more fall happened when David was here and his British Columbia friend came to see him. We all went to Anthony's for supper (and champagne!). A bit dizzy, John went to the rest room and lost his footing. This meant hours in the ER. In October '97 he had an extremely heavy nosebleed. Tim drove us to the ER again. In the back seat, I helped deal with the flow of blood.

Then in December, Tim, John, and I had our very last time in the ER—all night. He was finally admitted to the hospital with pneumonia. A few days later when antibiotics had brought that under control, an ambulance took him to the Stanford rehab center again, to meet his final, sadly unsuccessful, struggle.

Tim and I spent hours with him, seeing his animation gradually fade. He lost interest in TV and conversation. His eyes were usually fixed on the beautiful trees and shrubbery right outside his window. For a couple of days, a nurse came to John's bed and worked with me to improve my ability to get him out of bed. We practiced without much success.

I remembered from John's previous time in Stanford, after he broke his hip, that they had a custom of inviting the patient's family to attend a weekly staff meeting in which they shared plans for each patient's recovery. When I arrived on the scheduled day, I found that this wouldn't happen for John: he would not live long.

A wonderfully kind hospice woman there explained what would come. She brought me much comfort and assured me that before the end, I would get a call. When the time came, Tim and I sat by John's bed until his breathing gradually stopped, December 9, 1997.

We celebrated his life in a beautiful memorial service at the clubhouse here at Lake Jennings. Ned Wight, my Unitarian minister, gave generously of his time and ideas to help the children and me plan the farewell. They and some grandchildren took part in the ceremony and music. Golf buddies and other friends contributed memories of good times. So did a picture display.

It was such a blessing to have Tim with us during John's final weeks. Without him, I don't know how we could have avoided need for a nursing home. Before going to work in the morning, he helped get John out of bed, to his chair, and to the shower chair. He widened the door to the bathroom so the walker could go through. Mostly, we just loved having him here.

Tim's presence wasn't the only good thing that made John's final years go better. Equipment helped, for example, a commode with a removable part that could fit over the regular toilet seat to make it higher. After he broke his hip, he had a hospital bed. He didn't have his sleep interrupted so much after I hooked a urinal onto the commode with a bucket underneath. As time went on he could no longer handle that procedure and we used pads.

Other procedures became necessary during the final weeks. In addition to suggestions left by nurses, helpful tips came from Freddie, a marvelous woman here in the park. I still have several pages in which she tells how she was caring for her husband's needs during his dying months. She understood so well how it was for me, for her days were much the same as mine. One page told a variety of ways she managed to keep her spirits up. Remarkably, she continued doing what she had been doing for many years—and still does. She leaves cards at the homes of people in the park who are sick or who have lost a loved one.

For as long as possible after he had recovered fairly well from the effects of the major stroke, John enjoyed golf more than anything else. I took him to the golf course where he rode around with friends. While he did that, I went to the good library just a few steps away. Sometimes I walked through the nearby attractive neighborhoods of San Carlos. Once I went partly up Cowles Mountain.

John's favorite television programs were golf games. He was an ardent fan of Tiger Woods. He also liked audiotapes. He listened to every one of my series of sixty lectures on American history. When he finished the last one shortly before his death, I asked him, "What would you like me to get for you now?" His answer: "I want to hear them all over again."

I bought a book of card games for two. We liked best one that required few cards but was so well designed that it continued being fun to play. We also did the daily crossword puzzles. I had never cared for them before, but now I did enjoy working with John. He knew the words often used to make them come out right. I used some words John didn't know and enjoyed using our big unabridged dictionary. We made a good team. It was lonely without him.

# IN THE MEANTIME

For a couple of years, I volunteered to do a bit of teaching in the River Valley Charter School, two half-hour groups on Tuesday and another two on Friday. When I had read about this tiny experimental school in the newspaper, I was so intrigued that I offered to share some of my old material on writing better sentences before throwing it away. Also, I wanted to find a happy home for my English books, so as to help get rid of a lot of accumulated stuff to save my kids the trouble when I leave the scene.

I enjoyed working with high school kids again and I liked the philosophy of the man and his wife who started this school. They wanted to build a school where kids could avoid the kind of peer pressure they'd get in a high school of 2000 students. They started with a class of freshmen, some of whom had been home schooled. As they became sophomores, a new class of freshmen would come. Parents were expected to be actively involved with homework and the school.

Ten years after the first Straubinger reunion in San Diego, we were hosts again in June 1997, Donna having the traditional welcome barbecue Friday night, the main event here in the clubhouse Saturday night, and the Sunday picnic under Judy's big tree out in La Jolla.

In the meantime, our children were living their own lives. I start with Tim. After he returned from service in the Navy, he worked in the Golden Arrow dairy along with John until he was employed by the city of El Cajon, where he was able to use what he had learned in the submarine corps, skills used in plumbing, carpentry, electricity. These skills were also useful when he bought a small house and gave it a vigorous overhaul.

But then he dreamed of a large place farther out. He found one in Harbison Canyon and bought it in spite of misgivings because of the fire hazard in that area. I told my sisters about it in the Robin:

> Tim is finally into his "new" house after all sorts of snags before escrow could close. He has a nice pool, a fair view, lots of land, and a big house, but what a mess! He wanted a "fixer-upper" and that's what he got. He was reluctant for us to see it until he had worked on it, but we said if we didn't see the "before" picture, we couldn't fully appreciate the "after." His visions of a complete remodel seemed realistic only because we had seen the extensive modifications he had made to his previous place, knocking out and adding walls, moving the furnace, shifting fixtures in the kitchen and bath.
>
> He is planning to marry a nice young lady he met at work, Emily. Both are happy. He has stopped drinking and says he is going to check into a stop-smoking program at Kaiser as soon as the worst of the moving is over. (He did.)

By the time their first baby arrived, he had transformed the house into a place of safety and beauty. Emily brought her fine living room furniture; Judy gave them an antique chest of drawers; I gave them the Design Center table made to fit the Anza house. Tim constructed a room for the nursery.

Little Tara was more than welcome. I had written in the 1989 Round Robin: "Good news! Tim and Emily are going to have a baby. I hope they let us cuddle it a lot because it has been an awfully long time since we have had a wee one around ..."

Then came a whisper of a less joyful future when later in the year I wrote: "Tim's Emily is expecting her baby any day now. I feel sad that she is so standoffish, even with her mother, who calls me for long talks about her bafflement. We both are eagerly awaiting the baby and hoping Emily's isolationist attitude will lessen and we will get to share the joy."

Well, we did partly share the joy. I gave a shower and relished all the times of grandmotherly enjoyment that were given to me. I wrote:

Tim and Emily's baby arrived November 16, the day after Tim's birthday. Her name is Tara Jeanette and she is an active little bundle. I have seen her four times: a few minutes in the hospital, for a minute when Emily drove by the courthouse at lunchtime when I was on jury duty, for a short time when Tim and Emily brought her by on their way to town and then at her home when we shared a supper there.

I had a perfectly wonderful time with baby Tara when she was fussing a little and I rocked her in my arms and sang to her. She looked into my eyes for a long time. I loved every minute. I don't know whether she was enjoying the "music" or whether she was expressing amazement that anyone could make such a raucous, croaking sound! We are going to be privileged to babysit when Tim and Emily go to a play soon.

Their daughter Chelsi was born the day before Halloween in 1992, shortly before one of the most stressful times of my life. John had a very bad stroke requiring weeks of therapy after hospital and convalescent treatment. I was suffering severe back trouble at the time.

By August of the following year, however, our problems had eased enough that we could celebrate the little ones. I wrote: "Sunday Tim brought his family and did some chores for us. I wish you could have seen his two little girls. I've never seen anything more delightful than the way Tara plays with Chelsi and gets her laughing. Tara is trying to stop sucking her thumb. Chelsi is about the best-natured, happiest, most sociable baby ever."

There were other happy times for a few years, sometimes watching them frolic at home, dance to music here after a family party, or when sharing a special occasion at their church. But then late in 1996:

I hate to write about the bad thing that happened since my last letter. Early in September, Tim and Emily had a fight that ended with his leaving home, at least for a time. He is staying with us and sometimes with Judy or Donna.

He is bearing up well. He is a joy to have around. He does the supper dishes (after eating like a thresher!) Also, he fixes things and does yard work. He helps John and me with the daily cross-words and he is a first-rate conversationalist. He blames himself for overreacting and for having made bad choices, but he loves his two little girls, making him a prisoner in the entanglement.

Twice while Tim was still living with John and me, he brought home copies of letters commending him for his work with the City of El Cajon. The 1996 letter from the manager of recreation services thanked him for his exemplary "can do" approach to work requests, "timely, neat, professional. Consistently projects that you complete look better than the requestor would envision possible when requesting the work to be done."

His 1997 supervisor wrote a long letter to the Director of General Services and the city manager expressing appreciation for the maintenance team and especially Tim Straubinger:

> As you know, the Recreation Department is heavily involved in the International Friendship Festival. One of my responsibilities is the signs and decorations for the festival. With this responsibility, I needed to construct a new marquee for each stage. This marquee needed to be visible as well as sturdy. Because I am not construction oriented, I needed help and expertise in this area.

(He asked the crew leader for help in how to make it sturdy enough to withstand winds, etc. He was sent to Tim who gave him advice on the type of wood, went along to Home Depot to get it, and brought finished marquees two days later. The rest of the letter describes the reaction.)

> The quality of workmanship and the ingenious construction is unbelievable. I honestly cannot do justice in describing the marquees that Tim built. The professionalism that I was shown and the quality product that I received deserve applause. It is not often that you get such high cooperation between departments, and many municipal employees do not care about the quality of work they produce. This is not true with the facilities maintenance department or Tim Straubinger.

I wish Mother could have read this! One of her rare critical comments had to do with pre-school Tim's neglect of the waste baskets: I was too easy on him; he should have more chores. I guess I was waiting until he did OK on that one.

Of course, Tim enjoys being appreciated, but when opportunity arose he had no interest in advancing to a more highly paid position with more money. He said he didn't want to boss anyone, nor get ahead in typical ways.

Mending his marriage with Emily proved impossible despite meetings with a succession of counselors, both together and separately. A legal settlement dealt with money matters and parental responsibilities, but Tim was unable to arrange much follow-through on visits with his daughters. When he did bring them to see me, I gave Tara a piano lesson or two. Once, Gail's daughter Jessica joined Tara and Chelsi for a day with me. Nothing could be more delightful than watching the three of them play together.

Hoping that if he had his own place he could have more time with the girls than would be allowed here in the adult park, Tim rented a tiny house on the back lot of a property his friend Bill had just bought nearby in Santee. This fascinating place, now abandoned, had previously been lived in by several young men, one in a tent, one in a trailer, one in a tree house, and another in the geodesic dome which Tim now rented.

One fellow was a nursery worker who brought home quantities of plants no longer saleable but providing loads of good topsoil and growing well enough to allow for ingenious landscaping. We entered the place on a path beneath a leafy bower. Tropical foliage bordered the path; a koi pond was alongside.

Tim quickly arranged his tiny dome into a miniature kitchen nook and attractive, comfortable living quarters. He put into working order a solar water heater serving the outside homemade shower stall. He made plans for an annex to provide sleeping quarters in case the daughters were to visit.

Before this came about, however, Bill decided to sell. Then Tim bought a motor home, dreaming of vacations in the mountains or desert and of footloose retirement later on in his favorite places. Meanwhile, he rented an RV lot in the Viejas Indian reservation near the house he had turned over to Emily and the girls.

When David had a family, he no longer wanted to tour with the Indianapolis Symphony Orchestra; instead, he went to work in the basement of his home in Southport, just south of Indianapolis. He and Helen bought this green-shuttered, New England-style house when they saw it pictured in a newspaper ad. He sent me that clipping. When I took it to school and showed it to friends Paul and Dave, Dave exclaimed, "I know that house! It's right around the corner from my mother's house!" On my first trip there, I walked over and visited with her.

David undertook a wide variety of jobs. He developed a mail-order business selling the oboe reeds he made with cane imported from France. He repaired woodwind instruments sent to him by mail and brought to him by local musicians he knew from the orchestra and Jordan School of Music. He drove to Indiana University in Bloomington to bring home even more instruments to work on. The local school district employed him to condition their instruments.

To do all this work, he designed tools and machines and had them made or improved by machinists on whom he relied to turn his ideas into workable devices. How to make a better flute became an obsession, so he investigated how to go about making them by hand. A flute maker from Boston helped him get started and then became a lifelong friend.

Flute players must keep renewing felt pads that gradually lose their ability to keep air from getting through and interfering with the sound. David tried a myriad of different materials and structures to make pads that last longer and do a better job. At last, he developed an intricate design and specifications to do that. He got a patent for this pad and later on for clarinet and piccolo pads as well.

One of the advantages of doing this work at home was that he was there when the children came home from school. Helen would often still be at work as a teacher of stringed instruments and orchestra in junior high. She was also taking courses to upgrade her teaching skills, eventually earning her doctor's degree and employment as a school administrator.

Finding space for a growing number of machines, for storage needs, and for other equipment made the basement more and more crowded. What to do? There was no good way to add on to the house, and though there was plenty of land in the corner lot, expense for a large building would be prohibitive and the zoning probably wouldn't allow it. Then one day his part-time secretary said, "Hey, David, a podiatrist near me has put his place up for sale. Why don't you go have a look at it?"

He did. He bought it, moved in, and added a factory room about the size of a double garage where he could install large machines required for mass production of pads. The reception room, rest room, and mini-kitchen were made to order for David's business. Cubicles for patients became offices, space for putting flute components together, and a mailing room for Tuit, the employee who had emigrated from Vietnam.

Not long after this, I was able to go and admire David's jewel of a property, the acre-plus that stretches from a side street to a four-lane highway, a radical contrast to the dense virgin forests that border the side of the lot. This wooded area goes all the way from the highway to the side street, which faces a ten-car parking lot and the office/factory.

First, one comes into the entrance. Through an open window, clients and visitors could speak with Lisa (later Sue) sitting at her computer. They could wait in club chairs and admire a colorful collection of ceramic bowls and platters made by a local artist. I was dazzled by the factory, its awesome array of machinery, the intricacy of flute pad construction, and the ingenuity required to put it all together. How it had grown since he was a lone inventor working in a basement! But now he employs several helpers to produce the pads he patented and the flutes he makes to sell all over the world.

The property also includes a spacious, attractive house facing the busy highway but well back from the traffic noise. Until Joel and his family bought a house of their own, they lived in it, just a few steps from his job. Joel has always been involved in his father's work. Now he does much of the flute making.

David's marriage to Helen ended when they grew apart, she in pursuit of her teaching career and degree while he was absorbed in his inventions. David moved into the house.

A world map hanging in the hall of the office shows with pegs all the countries where David has customers. The "straubingerflutes.com" website gives addresses for repairmen in every country. Because high quality handmade flutes are made one at a time, they are quite expensive and usually attract no more orders than can be produced. Repair work, however, is more prolific.

A 2003 Round Robin says that:

> David has almost more work than he can handle. Though his profit margin is tiny, he enjoys making his far-flung customers happy. Last week, he had an SOS call for repairing the clarinet

of an Indianapolis Symphony player, son of Abba Eban. Who besides Irene knows who that is?

The main flutist in the Finland Symphony saved money for years to have David make him a gold flute. But first, he had the local repairman install David's pads on his old flute and make some improvements he had learned in one of David's seminars. He was so delighted with the result that he cancelled plans for the gold flute and used the money to pay off his mortgage!

By far, the pads market is now the major part of the business. Because pads must be installed properly, they are sold only to repairmen David qualifies in workshops he holds in Europe and sometimes in his home. Last year he held one in South Africa. In these workshops, he also teaches repair techniques, learning a few from his students along the way. Hundreds of travel and dwelling plans would probably be impossible to arrange were it not for the internet and David's partner Dale Simmons.

How Dale became part of the Straubinger family is a story of amazing coincidence. She and John met when they were both using walkers for exercise on the street in front of our houses. John was recovering from a stroke, Dale from brain surgery. They joked about having a walker race. We invited her to family dinners and became fast friends. She and David met here during visiting time after John's memorial service. Years later when David was here for a short visit they renewed their acquaintance. Mutual love for music led to friendship as they kept the phone lines busy. Eventually, friendship ripened and they became a committed couple. Dale had retired from her position as a Navy financial officer in San Diego. Her skills as a money manager, as an adept internet user, and as a writer made a perfect supplement to David's abilities as an inventor and teacher of repairmen. She divides her time between her Lake Jennings house and the Indiana house with David. Computers here, in the shop, and in the house are all programmed to do business work and are interconnected. This makes it possible for Dale to do company work when she is here to continue health care treatment with her Kaiser doctors.

Many of her problems were caused or made worse when she was badly hurt in an automobile accident. As soon as possible, she came here for treatment. For a while there was a bad mistake. Somehow X-ray results given to her Dr. Z. were wrong and she was referred to therapists for exercises which made the pain and injury worse. Dale credits a therapist with realizing this and rescuing her from this dreadful detour. Her intercession led to surgery. The surgeon, Dr. O'Hara, said that torn, smashed muscles, tendons and bone made an even worse mess than the MRI had shown.

The slightest movement of the mending shoulder had to be prevented, so she was confined by a wide strap and sling. She couldn't be alone at all, but danger of infection caused Dr. Z. to rule out hospital or nursing home care. Dale's daughter came for five days; David took over for a while. I took it from there. It's uncanny how well she holds up, endures pain, and insists on always looking her best. When Dr. O'Hara first saw her—before learning the true situation—he didn't believe she had much wrong with her and delayed surgery for months. Then came an about-face. "Schedule immediately" became his order.

She still has problems with various internal injuries, to say nothing of problems remaining after a dentist pulled the wrong tooth! Her extensive and severe injuries require the continuity of care she gets with a doctor she trusts and who knows her history. She is amazingly pain-tolerant and determined to carry on with business tasks and with projects she sets for herself, like taking digital pictures and DVDs for relatives and friends. She borrowed my drawer full of pictures and memorabilia to create a beautiful album and had it published as a gift for my ninetieth birthday. She ordered additional copies for family members.

Judy continues to be my only child who is usually nearby and there for me when I need her. Every morning she used to phone to see if I was all right, until I started wearing a pendant for calling a security service in case I should fall and be unable get up. She is always ready with transportation if necessary.

On game night—usually every Wednesday—she and occasionally Juliet come here for supper, talk, and play our favorite games Rummikub, Scrabble, and Anagrams. I have a chance to cook things I wouldn't make for myself alone; she does the dishes. A typical comment as she leaves is "Thanks for letting me win." My constant answer: "I didn't LET you win!" (P.S. We both win.)

Her health has been good except for thyroid surgery and medication, and for tooth repair after a fall in which she fractured her left arm while her right wrist was still in a cast. She has often been hostess for gatherings in her unique back yard, especially on Easter or special birthdays.

Music has been a constant part of her life. Her violin provides one of the few musical careers that continue well into the usual retirement age. It's flexible: one can do as much or as little as one chooses. Judy gives lessons and plays either her violin or viola in the San Diego Chamber Orchestra and in a string quartet that plays for weddings, church programs and other events. She was pleased to be a substitute in the San Diego Symphony Orchestra when guest artist Jacqueline du Pres played the *Elgar Concerto*.

Her quartet once played in a restaurant that charged $80 for a lavish four-course dinner, serving delicacies in the menus served on the Titanic before it went down. Tickets were sold out well in advance. The string quartet was employed to play all through the dinner as musicians had done on the Titanic and in the movie.

Judy's geology courses and Tim's self-taught knowledge made for a most enjoyable trip for the three of us on the way to the final Straubinger reunion in Colorado Springs. When I was able to break in with a question, I'd ask, "What caused that formation?" or some other ignorant query.

For a few of the later twentieth-century years, Donna too lived nearby. She and Wayne moved from their El Cajon house when they retired to a prefab they bought and had constructed on the outskirts of Lone Pine at the foot of Mt. Whitney, the highest mountain in continental U.S. When I first entered the front door and looked through the dining area toward the kitchen, I gasped, "WOW!" Filling the window frame was a striking view of that beautiful snow-covered mountain.

The Gruenewald acre abuts Alabama Hills, an area filled with unique, huge boulders, oddly placed, which present those who drive through with weird, fantastic formations around every corner. This is the locale where many western movies were made. Every year the Lone Pine Film Museum has a festival in which some of these old movies are shown. Donna works in the museum sometimes.

A few miles north lies the site of Manzanar, one of the internment camps where Japanese residents, even citizens, were confined during World War II. It is now a state park with a building in which the history of the encampment is depicted with films, artifacts, and shelter replicas. Whole families had often been crowded into one room. Visitors can walk through the grounds to see road signs and lot patterns, though everything else is gone except for one of the places where talented Japanese gardeners were able to accomplish miracles in making islands of beauty for this dreary place. I stood a long time admiring this spot, wondering at the difficulties they had been forced to experience and what they must have been thinking about America.

One of my most cherished books is one published in 1946 that I bought years ago: *Citizen 13660*. Reprinted, I suppose, copies were for sale in the park store. I had almost worn out my copy by lending it and by reading it several times, marveling at how well the writer's simple drawings and text had depicted make-do life in her camp as she recorded it day by day. I was awed by the fact that there was not one hint of bitterness in her writing. Surely she must have felt enraged!

Donna and Wayne come south every few weeks to visit Gail's family and me, to see their dentist, and to buy groceries and supplies that aren't available in Lone Pine. They see doctors in a neighboring city to treat Wayne for the Parkinson's disease he has developed in recent years. Sometimes they fish in lakes they remember from the years they lived in Bishop, about fifty miles north of Lone Pine.

Quilting has become Donna's main activity. A quilting group in Lone Pine and another in Bishop turns out scores of unusual designs, patterned with unusual fabrics. She has made baby quilts for her son Karl's children, Collin and Anya, and for her daughter Gail's child, Jessica, and Gail's stepchildren. For my ninetieth birthday, she created a large, colorful quilt full of family pictures that had been printed onto fabric.

Gail is now married to Mark Mikels. Years ago, her husband Craig, Jessica's father, took his boat to go fishing in the ocean, but didn't come back. When the empty boat came to shore, the Coast Guard went looking for him. Why he was overboard and how he drowned is a mystery.

With few exceptions, I review the history of my descendants with pleasure. At this point, Judy, Donna, David, and Tim are doing what they want to do and are independent, healthy enough, and blessed with children of their own. Judy has Juliet; Donna has Karl and Gail; David has Joel and Melissa; Tim has Tara and Chelsi.

One of my greatest pleasures is seeing how well my children relate to one another. As they were growing up, they must have quarreled as siblings usually do, but now have only affection for each other. Their father's temperament may have something to do with it. I tell them, "The best thing I ever did for you was to pick you a good father." I am only sorry that their marriages didn't last. Only Donna and Wayne can celebrate their golden wedding anniversary as John and I did. I pray that Wayne survives his unfortunate Parkinson's affliction.

I am awed by the number of additional descendants I can call my own. Not only do I have seven grandchildren, but also seven great grandchildren: Melissa's Jonathan and Anna; Joel's Maddy and Evelyn; Karl's Collin and Anya; and Gail's Jessica. All beautiful children. I wish for them a less troublesome world than the one I'll be leaving them.

# MILLENIUM!

The new century found me in reasonable good shape, except for a painful right knee that no longer likes to walk. In June, 2000, I wrote in the Robin, "Yes, Irene, it's better to say, 'I'm fine, with a grin, than to let the folks know the shape we're in.' With good friends and sisters we do need to share commiseration, but with others like grocery clerks, etc. who say 'How are you?' without really wanting to know, I always say, 'Good enough, thank you.' Once I took the liberty of giving advice to a neighbor who always overdoes her answer to 'How are you?': I suggested that Doris answer 'So-so.' Myrtle often used the answer: 'My get up and go has got up and went.' Apt!"

Before the next letter, I had undergone surgery to replace my bad knee. The operation itself wasn't too stressful, even though I had a pain block instead of general anesthetic and could therefore hear alarming sounds from down there: the noise of pounding, sawing as they took the bad knee out. I must have been given a tranquilizer as well, for I wasn't horrified, only fascinated. After the surgery, I was able to squeeze a bulb to bring pain relief down from the bag above my bed. The healing process was worse.

The September letter said that I could still say "Good enough" but I wished I could be confident that I'd get back to functioning as well as before. "At least I'm back to typing and to playing the piano. I started driving after four weeks. I shop and I've started using my exercise bike.

Twice a week, I go to therapy class and do my painful knee exercises two or three times a day with the aid of fewer pain pills. Progress, I guess."

In February 2001, I said, "My knee is still ouchy," in May, "My knee doesn't change much: they say it takes a year, but maybe I'll always have arthritis there. I walk about a mile a day, spread out sometimes."

Our letters dealt with more important topics than our declining health. For example: "Edna, you mentioned the old backhouse. Have you ever wondered about the agonizing situation of refugees and other people in primitive situations and how they manage when they don't have even Sears catalogs? When I think of how much toilet paper I use here, all alone, I wonder who sends truckloads to Kosovo, for example."

In addition to these letters to my sisters, I usually write other accounts of my travels, like the plane trip to Karl's wedding. He had urged me to come, but I was reluctant to fly with that painful knee. Without even asking for it, however, the alert Southwest workers provided me with wheelchair transportation all the way to Indiana. David would be with me from then on. We drove to St. Louis, where the couple had met, where Chanda's relatives lived, and where the wedding took place.

We stayed in a motel during several days of getting to know the bride, her family, and friends. I wrote,

> How gratifying to find Karl marrying into a really fine family! I was pleased to hear that Chanda's chosen mission is to be a doctor to "underserved children." As a pediatrician, she had interned in Africa, trying to help horribly sick babies and youngsters dying of AIDS. I had recently viewed an account of this tragedy on a Frontline special. Drug companies resist providing cheaper versions of remedies they had developed. And I had been appalled when Bush II had cut off efforts at prevention provided by Planned Parenthood.
>
> I enjoyed visiting with Chanda's intelligent mother. Too bad I won't see her again; I would love having her for a friend. Amusingly, she gave one-of-a-kind names for her three, Chanda, Tovy, and Jad. As a teacher she knew the problems of too many kids with the same popular names.
>
> The wedding next day was beautiful. Chanda, of course, was the star in her off-white long satin gown, full and slim-bodiced.

Whether it was the setting or the music, especially the "Ode to Joy" from Beethoven's ninth symphony, by the time the procession came down the aisle, I was teary-eyed. Jessica was the flower girl, her mother Gail and Chanda's brother Jad recited readings from the scripture and Kahlil Gibran. The woman pastor gave a sermon on the meaning of the beatitudes.

At the reception dinner, I had the good fortune to be seated next to Ushma Shah, a vital, intelligent young woman who came to the U.S. with her parents as a small child from India. I have never had a more stimulating conversation about educational matters than with Ushma. She was finishing her studies at Harvard with an ambitious and idealistic goal: she aims to become superintendent working with principals in an urban school district. What a mission!

We traded ideas about the almost insurmountable obstacles to improving inner city schooling. I was surprised to find that we were thinking along many of the same lines. I have rarely found anyone so willing to acknowledge that a drastic, fundamental systemic change is required. Palliative measures won't be enough. Money alone won't help. Neither will vouchers nor too-soon testing. There must also be something done about housing and financing patterns.

Incentives must be attractive enough to lure the most skillful, experienced teachers into places where ability is most needed. Understandably, beginning teachers are apt to burn out before they have learned how to do a good job. Or, if they do hang on, they will earn enough priority to gain transfer to the suburbs where life is easier.

I enjoyed riding with David to St. Louis from Indiana and afterward to and from Ohio. I exulted in miles and miles of green spaces empty of almost everything except for dense forests lining the freeway. When I was growing up in Ohio, woods were being cut down to make more space for growing grain. For some reason, farmers stopped doing that and were letting trees grow back. What a treat it was to see the area looking as unspoiled as if we immigrants had never come.

David's delicious selection of CDs by contemporary composers made the four-hour trip even more delightful. Some were played by musicians who were friends of his in Eastern Europe. Music had thrived behind the iron curtain, he had discovered.

That was on Sunday, but when we returned from Ohio on a weekday, we had a much different experience. It was quite a driving challenge, for there was much heavy roadwork going on. Multitudes of bulldozers and other monster rigs clogged lanes all along the "freeway." Three years before when I came through here on another weekday, the same picture gave me the notion that we would be treated to more lanes or smoother surfaces as the result of all this activity. But no, as David pointed out, year-round truck traffic and freezing weather take such a toll on surfaces that maintenance itself demands intensive work during the only months it's possible.

More than ever, I deplore the growing excess of big trucks. On a stretch of freeway from Findlay to Bowling Green, I could count as many as a dozen trucks lined up single-file, going the same speed, of course, though occasionally one would dart out to try getting ahead, clogging the single lane available for cars.

Another time, we came to a railroad crossing just as a warning bell signaled the approach of about thirty freight cars. I clapped and said to David, "What if we had cars and trucks first, before trains? Then when we saw those overbearing, heavy monsters all lined up and going the same speed, we would have said, "Why not hook them all together and make a special track for them so as to save all that tire rubber, the time of bored drivers—and the roads!?"

We had a memorable reunion in Bowling Green, where we met cousins Doug and Meg. On their way down from Dundee, Michigan, they had picked up his mother Evelyn in Toledo. David, Alyce, and I collected our cousin Martha in Findlay. The seven of us enjoyed lunch and non-stop exuberant talk until three at a most accommodating restaurant. Though they usually close at two, they urged us to stay put at our round table. "No bother," they said. A final visit for some of us?

On the way back to Alyce's, we stopped at the nursing home to visit her husband Gene. In his wheelchair, he met us with a beaming smile just inside the door. He understands whatever we say, but in response he can only gesture, along with frustrating attempts at speech. The "dough, dough, dough" sound is all he can manage. Tears as we leave. So heartbreaking, such a vigorous, confident man before the stroke!

On previous trips to Ohio after Gene's stroke, I had been dismayed by his inability to realize that he was not saying what he thought he was saying. He'd give special stress to that "dough, dough, dough," trying to make us understand. Once I tried a therapist's suggestion that we record a conversation and play it back to him so he'd hear himself as we heard him. I took a tape recorder and tried that, but it didn't work. I also made some cards with pictures from a book of sign-language gestures, two alike for the benefit of whoever was helping him. No sale.

My experience with helpful airline attendants on the flight to Indiana and Karl's wedding gave me courage to fly once more. I had read about how well Jet Blue treated their passengers, so I asked Dale to get me an internet ticket to Ft. Myers, Florida, the nearest airport to Aunt Naomi. Sure enough, the trip went perfectly, a direct flight to New York, an easy connecting flight, and then a limousine driver waiting to take me to the Ft. Charlotte motel Dale had reserved for me.

In a rented car, Naomi and I shopped, explored, lunched by a window with a wonderful view, and savored two suppers in a Chinese buffet that offered unusual, delicious selections. One afternoon we sat reminiscing in a pergola outside the retirement home, laughing as we watched the way a mama duck took charge of her lively ducklings as they waddled down to a pool, and a pair of squirrels quarreling their way up a nearby tree. I loved that week with Naomi; she is so dear to me. We knew that this would be our last time together, except for the Robin and the telephone.

Two paragraphs in my August 2003 letter tell about a minor problem with my car and a major problem for a good friend and neighbor:

> Monday I was in Alpine with a group of friends. As I was backing out of the parking area, I saw a look of concern on the faces of others who were about to get into their cars. I rolled down my window to ask why, and then I heard for myself a loud clanking from the hood of my car.
>
> After an hour or so spent in calling State Farm road service and a few towing companies, my car and I were hauled to Tom the Faithful who diagnosed the racket. It was something in the air conditioning system. Goodbye, a thousand dollars: other things had to be done to comply with new standards for air conditioners. I now await a phone call saying someone is bringing Old Faithful

Volvo home. Aged as she is (21), Tom says she is in good shape otherwise.

The other paragraph tells about the difficult time I had trying to locate Eleanor in a hospital after a freak accident.

> She is a dear neighbor who doesn't drive but gets around in the park with a top-of-the-line golf cart her son bought her. When she didn't show up at yoga yesterday, I learned that another golf cart driver had hit the power button rather than the brake and had collided with Eleanor. Eventually I reached someone who told me that she had fortunately not broken her pelvis and back as expected, just three ribs and the sternum but was in intensive care to guard against pneumonia.

> What a downer! A few years ago, she told me about her awful years when Hitler moved into Czechoslovakia, grabbed her husband for his army, and left the women to fend for themselves. It had meant terribly long walks, hunger, and other hardships for the refugees. After a long time, Eleanor and her husband settled down a few houses from me. I used to see him walking painfully along the street with his walker. After he died, Eleanor concentrated on the magnificent flower beds all around her house. Sometimes after yoga, she stopped by for a visit with me. Once I started writing an account of her experiences, but before we got to the most harrowing part again, 9/11 happened and frightened her so badly that her son told her to never again talk of her past experiences.

Between that August letter and the next one in November there were two destructive events. I mentioned the car accident in the section about David and Dale. In the same October month came another disaster: the fire! I wrote that

> I couldn't begin to describe the horror of it, the deaths, the hundreds of houses burned down, the scarred and ugly hillsides. Tim's house in Harbison Canyon burned to the ground. Emily and the girls are with her new boyfriend and she is looking for a house to rent. With two dogs, it can't be an apartment. Lots of luck! Prices are simply unbelievable. Even though they have good insurance, I can't imagine its being enough.

> I had gone to the bathroom about 3:00 Saturday night and

looked out the front window to see a long line of fire beyond the farthest ridge. In the past when fires had come even closer, they had been put out rather quickly; so I went back to bed. In the morning I could see nothing but heavy smoke. As I learned later, smoke hides flames right behind it, so I had no idea the fire was close. I was glued to the TV for news about areas like Ramona, "far away" places, and wasn't even dressed when I heard a siren right outside my house and a bullhorn yelling, "Leave at once!" I yanked on my clothes, grabbed my purse, pills, keys, and a few picture albums, and went to Donna's in El Cajon, before the traffic jam got too bad.

When I returned the next day, I saw that the two houses directly below me were demolished. On wooden doorsteps leading to my front door was a twig with charred leaves. It had blown over from a bush at the side of the house. That bush was also full of charred leaves. A fortunate coincidence: only two months ago, I had tree men cut down the tall pine tree in my front yard. What a dangerous fire trap it would have been! Some park residents put out just such a fire, started by burning embers beside the clubhouse.

About a month later smoke and ashes were still heavy. I had written the above account but hadn't mailed it. Now I added another page:

On this morning's walk I saw that workmen had made considerable progress in piling up remains of the two burned houses into dump trucks. The other day, I asked them how many of those huge dumpsters it would take. "Five." On a later walk, I asked one of the onlookers, "Where do you live?" Pointing to the rubble, she said, "It *was* there!" After I threw my arms around her in sympathy, I listened to her long story. Like the rest of us, she had been evicted from the park when the fire got close. Next day as she came back and headed up the street toward her home she saw for the first time the mess that had been her house and that of her next-door neighbor. Imagine the shock!

Atop a surviving metal cable box, she had lined up four small doo-dads she had rescued from the ashes. She told me in detail how she had tried to clean them with Brillo pads, etc. It was so touching. Fortunately, there was an empty house right down the street, so she and her husband immediately moved in. A couple of women took over the job of getting them settled: they sent around a flyer asking for donations and/or loans of furniture. In March a prefab was installed by the same company that would soon build one for Donna and Wayne.

Tim spent many hours after the fire trying to get the best possible insurance settlement for the destroyed house, which he had given, except for a relatively small payment, to Emily as part of the separation settlement. It was lucky that he was within months of paying off his Cal-Vet loan and was therefore insured by that policy. Nevertheless, it took him many hours of negotiating before he was able to establish a good replacement price by preparing a complete list of specifications.

For a few years, my replaced knee made it possible for me to renew my morning walks around the block. Nothing cheered me like an autumn walk to enjoy rain-washed green hills and reddening liquidambars. Some evenings there was a glorious sunset. Like a pageant, it would go so fast that I had to catch it quickly. When my other knee complained too much, I had to gradually give up these daily walks. For a while I kept track of how it was going, by jotting down grades: C, B-, C+, D. I continued weekly yoga sessions for a while.

My nurse friend Audrey went with me to help evaluate with a surgeon whether I should undergo another surgery. He said my age, in the late eighties, didn't necessarily rule it out so I didn't—at that time. He put me on a waiting list. I'd make a decision when the time came on whether to go ahead or to make do with ibuprofen, cortisone if necessary. When an opening finally arrived, I chose the "make do" route.

Only two painful but temporary problems with my good health from then on: a second bout with shingles and plantar fasciitis on my heel. Medications keep my blood pressure under control. Happily, my eyes are good enough for driving.

Friend and neighbor Barbara and I take turns driving to our Unitarian Universalist fellowship in Santee. I no longer play piano for services as I had done regularly for about ten years. This routine kept me practicing regularly, much more than I do now, though I still enjoy learning new music and keeping in touch with my favorite composers in compositions by Grieg, Debussy, Gershwin, Scriabin, Bach, Mozart, Beethoven, and other classics.

In earlier years, I participated in AAUW activities: a book club in which we all read the same book; another where I twice reviewed a book; a monthly group which went together to a movie, lunch, and discussion; and a monthly duplicate bridge group where we practiced advanced conventions by constructing examples on the duplicate boards.

When I dropped all that, I continued playing bridge with a UU group and with an intimate group of five that gets together regularly to improve our bidding and play and to chat. When I no longer wanted to drive at night, I stopped going to concerts in ECPAC (East County Performing Arts Center) or to symphony concerts in San Diego, except for an occasional Sunday afternoon concert.

Now comes the final Round Robin letter in my autobiography. In reading letters of earlier years, I feel as if I'm reading a novel about someone else's life. What a lot of selves one lives in ninety years! If my kids or grandkids aren't interested in my memories or these old letters, maybe a great, great grandchild will be a history buff like my nephew Douglas Heinlen and maybe my survivors won't have thrown my masterpiece away. Douglas has even done research to establish that he and I have the same grandfather as Edgar Allen Poe some five or six generations ago!

*May 10, 2005*
Dear Other Mothers (and Dear Aunts),

As a special gift to me on this Mothers Day, Tim agreed to go to church with me. It was pleasing to have my friends meet him and chat with him during coffee hour. Twice when David went with me, we played a piano/oboe duet, a Satie piece. Donna and Wayne had also visited. I'll try for Judy next year.

Afterward Tim and I had soup and salad on my patio, where it was nice and sunny, white clouds, blue sky overhead, Lake Jennings, El Capitan Mountain, and our golden wedding campground clearly visible. We could even see the cliff between ridges where my children had scattered their father's ashes.

I'm in the middle of a sorting-out, throwing-away project. I've been a true "clip-to-maniac" since LWV and teaching days, but now I think it's time to start discarding these clippings so as to save work for my heirs. My plan is to sort through one subject folder at a time and glance through them for anything worth copying on the computer before discarding it. Yesterday, I took a big sack full to the dump. I congratulate myself!

I am also pleased to have made a couple of decisions about the way to spend my remaining years. One: strictly avoid meetings wherein one goes to hear a lecture, book report or whatever, without plenty of time for discussion or just visiting afterward. I get plenty of information and opinion from my own readings or C-SPAN. I especially plan to avoid big groups. Yesterday there was a Mother's Day luncheon at the clubhouse, along with a fashion show, a silent auction of donated items, everyone dressed up, nice decorations, all well planned. But I realized it was all wasted on me and I slipped out soon and went home. With everyone talking it was a strain to hear even the ones next to me and I couldn't care less about a fashion show. Resolved: no more time wasting.

Two: I will rarely undertake driving to unfamiliar addresses. Twice in one week, I found myself lost in Spring Valley even though I thought I had planned the route exactly. Maps have their drawbacks, though I admit they did rescue me when I pulled to the side of the road to reconnoiter. (I had to look up the spelling for that, Irene.) Do you-all remember when Irene and I spelled down the whole high school? And to think, I used to be a proof-reader! Ah, how time changes.

For five weeks, I taped episodes of *Little House on the Prairie*. Then I erased the commercials and made copies, one for Tara and Chelsi and the other for the disabled daughter of a woman in my writing group. I can't think of any more good deeds, unless you count cooking good meals for Judy and Tim every Wednesday. Tonight we are going to set up the slide projector and view slides we haven't seen for years. (My birthday request.)

Christmas 2005 was unlike any Christmas-past in many ways. In the previous month, I'd felt rather uncomfortable as I kept thinking of cards I should be sending and gifts I might buy in spite of my family's resolve to abstain from shopping this year. For the first time, I skipped sending cards. My only trip to the stores was to buy a few books for 1½-year-old Collin. He would be here the day after Christmas with Karl and Chanda for three days. Naturally, I was busy clearing the decks for their arrival. The room with the foldout bed had to be cleared of piles of books and magazines. My Christmas tree consisted of a few dinky ornaments and a skimpy string of lights on my imitation palm tree.

All went well until Christmas Day. It was an unfamiliar route to Gail's home in Mira Mesa, so I printed in big black letters a list of streets and left or right turns. When I was about to turn left on Jade Coast, I was surprised to see that it led to an apartment complex, not a street. What a nuisance! I now saw that the sign said "Jade Coast Ct." for "Court," not "Jade Coast Dr." for "Drive." Moving slowly on, I quickly spotted the proper sign. The light was green; I turned left. A big mistake! I had been so accustomed to the left turn signals and/or familiar streets that I failed to notice the oncoming van. *Crash*! Within minutes, the police had phoned Gail. Judy, a few minutes behind me, had come along on her way to the Christmas dinner. Nobody was hurt; the car didn't look too bad. Ice packs and pain pills eased my pain from the impact of the seat belt. After three weeks, I was OK. I sold my faithful Volvo for $100, a great bargain for the salvage man because it had been in perfect condition before the accident.

Earlier in the year, Tim had helped Emily and his daughters get resettled. Though he managed to get a good price for the land and a good insurance settlement for the house, things were so expensive in this area that they decided to move to Silver City, New Mexico, not far from Emily's father. After renting an apartment for a while, she bought a fine house in a good neighborhood in Silver City. Tim drove over frequently to see his girls, to help get them settled, and to look around for a suitable location for himself when he retired. He looked forward to living near open spaces for him and his dog to explore. I rode over with him on the Thanksgiving holiday for a preview of his new environment with various places for sale.

Luckily for me, he hadn't moved yet when I wrecked my car. In January, he went with me to get a replacement. I decided on a Toyota Camry, a car with a good record for safety, my main requirement. That had been our primary reason for choosing a nearly new Volvo more than twenty years ago! I could have bought a car less gas thirsty, but I don't drive much and I wanted comfort and quick response on the freeway when I needed it. I feared that adjusting to a different car after twenty years with the old one would be stressful for a while. It wasn't.

Tim's high desert acre with a comfortable trailer suits him perfectly. It's on the continental divide at the edge of Silver City, adjacent to wild country, though he has two neighbors within shouting distance. Twice he came here, picked me up, and took me there for a few days. Every morning a mama deer and two youngsters came over and had breakfast on tall weeds and low-hanging juniper twigs. Once, a deer came within a yard of the window where I was sitting. We looked at each other a full minute before she walked away. Tim took me for drives and one Sunday to Silver City's tiny Unitarian/Universalist church.

Since the ride over there was not too taxing, I decided it wouldn't be too much of a strain on my aging carcass to ride an equal distance to see my northern-California relatives. In early 2007, Tim joined me and drove my car there. The ride was purely delightful as signs of spring were making varied countryside views even lovelier. At Pismo Beach Lynda's son joined us for supper beside the ocean. Then we enjoyed days with both sisters' families, with side trips, bridge for me, and hikes with Lynda for Tim. We went to a state park with Mary and walked along a trail to find a plaque about her daughter saying:

This trail is dedicated to the memory of Caroll Smith Knechle, Supervisor for the Sonoma County Probation Camp. Caroll's energy and enthusiasm were essential elements that contributed to the completion of numerous projects that serve the disabled and disadvantaged citizens of Sonoma County, including this trail which as been named in her honor.

# NINETY YEARS!

The year 2008 brought one pleasant event and one disaster. Coming home after supper at a local restaurant, David and Dale saw the business in flames with fire engines all around. Parts of the building were completely destroyed, the factory part damaged almost beyond repair, computers, finished pads and components gone, flute parts and tools covered with soot and ashes.

It took a small army of volunteers, friends, and employees to salvage what was worth saving. They gathered around a pool table in the basement of the house to clean and polish those tools and parts that debris would quickly erode if not removed. Insurance couldn't begin to cover the pain, the cost, and hours of stressful work required to save the business from collapse. As I write this, troubles are far from over. Worrisome health hazards have slowed neither David's nor Dale's determination to solve never-ending problems when they assert themselves.

That dreadful event happened months after the happy one, but I put it first to avoid letting misfortune end my narrative. Neither did I choose to postpone my memoirs however long it might take for their website to proclaim in headlines that all is well: "Straubinger Flutes Makes Full Recovery!" May it be soon.

I was struck by moments of unbelief when I beheld my four children and many other dear ones here in my house celebrating my ninetieth birthday. Could I possibly be ninety? But here they were and here was

I, actually ninety years old! On this joyous occasion I felt more like a little birthday girl being pampered by grown-ups. Women were out there in the kitchen—out-of-bounds for me—as they prepared platters of goodies.

My two darling California daughters and granddaughter Gail prepared tiny sandwiches, chips, dips, and punch, and decorated my house with crepe paper streamers, banners, balloons, and flowers. Gail reminded everyone that I didn't want gifts. Instead, she asked them to write notes on long narrow strips telling some memory of me. She hung them with tiny clothespins onto a beautifully decorated wreath. Seeing these colorful ribbons swaying in the breeze out there on the porch, little Collin (three years old) and Anya (one) insisted on writing theirs too! They had come with Karl and Chanda from Denver. David came from Indiana, Tim from New Mexico. Nephews Michael and Robert came with their families. Edna, Carl, Lynda, Bill, and their sons came. Myrl came with Judy and Juliet. It was all so heartwarming, as were many lovely cards.

Role reversal makes for several life style changes for old folks: instead of teaching our youngsters how to cook, now they *do* the cooking; instead of our concern for their safety, their concern is for our safety. Instead of our caring for them when they're sick, they come to our rescue or take us to a doctor when necessary. Sometimes, however, American society gives us more privileges than we deserve, like "senior citizen" discounts for expenses that we can afford more easily than young ones can. We vote more than they do to get more health care and tax advantages than are always justified.

Such reflections pass quickly as I sit watching this houseful of people enjoying each other. It's pleasing to be responsible for this reunion, never to be repeated as is. On the coffee table lies Dale's beautiful gift album containing pictures of past generations, while the several generations which fill my living room now present visions of the future–to a pivotal person: me!

I have only gratitude for my gift of life. Perhaps I could have made better use of that beautiful gift, but I was rewarded nevertheless with loving parents, sisters, husband, children and friends, with good enough health and a comfortable home in the best spot in the world.

I now set about a long delayed sorting/discarding task. I'll start with the cabinet of thirty-six 8½" by 11" metal drawers labeled with their contents: bills, IRS, letters, medical records, etc. Facetiously, I put a burial agreement with the memorial society in bottom right drawer, the very last, labeled *THE END!*